"YOU DON'T UNDERSTAND THE FIRST THING ABOUT ME—"

The script called for her to be pulled into his arms and kissed fiercely and Alex didn't hesitate. He grasped her and pulled her close to him and his mouth came down on hers, hard and punishing. She thrust her hands between them and struggled as the script directed, the unconscious part of her brain registering the cool firmness of his mouth on hers, the warm scent of his body, the lovely feel of his hard flesh under her hands . . . and then she was engaged in a desperate battle to keep from relaxing into his arms and returning his kiss with an urgent need of her own.

A CANDLELIGHT ECSTASY ROMANCE ®

74 CAPTIVE DESIRE, *Tate McKenna*
75 CHAMPAGNE AND RED ROSES, *Sheila Paulos*
76 COME LOVE, CALL MY NAME, *Anne N. Reisser*
77 MASK OF PASSION, *Kay Hooper*
78 A FATAL ATTRACTION, *Shirley Hart*
79 POWER PLAY, *Jayne Castle*
80 RELENTLESS LOVE, *Hayton Monteith*
81 BY LOVE BETRAYED, *Anne N. Reisser*
82 TO CATCH THE WILD WIND, *Jo Calloway*
83 A FIRE OF THE SOUL, *Ginger Chambers*
84 LOVE HAS NO MERCY, *Eleanor Woods*
85 LILAC AWAKENING, *Bonnie Drake*
86 LOVE TRAP, *Barbara Andrews*
87 MORNING ALWAYS COMES, *Donna Kimel Vitek*
88 FOREVER EDEN, *Noelle Berry McCue*
89 A WILD AND TENDER MAGIC, *Rose Marie Ferris*
90 BREATHLESS SURRENDER, *Kay Hooper*
91 SPELLBOUND, *Jayne Castle*
92 CRIMSON MORNING, *Jackie Black*
93 A STRANGE ELATION, *Prudence Martin*
94 A WAITING GAME, *Diana Blayne*
95 JINX LADY, *Hayton Monteith*
96 FORBIDDEN FIRES, *Nell Kincaid*
97 DANCE THE SKIES, *Jo Calloway*
98 AS NIGHT FOLLOWS DAY, *Suzanne Simmons*
99 GAMBLER'S LOVE, *Amii Lorin*
100 NO EASY WAY OUT, *Elaine Raco Chase*
101 AMBER ENCHANTMENT, *Bonnie Drake*
102 SWEET PERSUASION, *Ginger Chambers*
103 UNWILLING ENCHANTRESS, *Lydia Gregory*
104 SPEAK SOFTLY TO MY SOUL, *Dorothy Ann Bernard*
105 A TOUCH OF HEAVEN, *Tess Holloway*
106 INTIMATE STRANGERS, *Denise Mathews*
107 BRAND OF PASSION, *Shirley Hart*
108 WILD ROSES, *Sheila Paulos*
109 WHERE THE RIVER BENDS, *Jo Calloway*
110 PASSION'S PRICE, *Donna Kimel Vitek*
111 STOLEN PROMISES, *Barbara Andrews*
112 SING TO ME OF LOVE, *JoAnna Brandon*
113 A LOVING ARRANGEMENT, *Diana Blayne*

CAUGHT IN THE RAIN

Shirley Hart

A CANDLELIGHT ECSTASY ROMANCE ®

Published by
Dell Publishing Co., Inc.
1 Dag Hammarskjold Plaza
New York, New York 10017

ISBN: 0-440-10999-X

Printed in the United States of America
First printing—February 1983

To Our Readers:

We have been delighted with your enthusiastic response to Candlelight Ecstasy Romances®, and we thank you for the interest you have shown in this exciting series.

In the upcoming months we will continue to present the distinctive sensuous love stories you have come to expect only from Ecstasy. We look forward to bringing you many more books from your favorite authors and also the very finest work from new authors of contemporary romantic fiction.

As always, we are striving to present the unique, absorbing love stories that you enjoy most—books that are more than ordinary romance.

Your suggestions and comments are always welcome. Please write to us at the address below.

Sincerely,

The Editors
Candlelight Romances
1 Dag Hammarskjold Plaza
New York, New York 10017

CHAPTER ONE

With a deep sense of relief, Cathy Taylor closed her suitcase and glanced at her roommate. "I think I'm ready."

"I think you're crazy," Ellen replied drily.

Cathy's mouth curved in a smile as she combed her silky dark hair into loose curls around her shoulders. "Perhaps I am, but—don't remind me."

Ellen sighed. "Wade called again last night. Don't you know he's bound to give you a part in his next movie purely out of guilty conscience?"

"Then I'm sure the part wouldn't be right for me," Cathy answered emphatically and lowered the suitcase to the floor with a positive thump. "He has nothing to feel guilty about. I agreed to the divorce."

"What choice did you have?" Ellen argued. "He certainly wasn't hiding his infatuation for his new love. Everybody knew about her."

Pain crossed Cathy's face and Ellen immediately repented.

"Cathy, I'm sorry. I didn't mean . . . look, I just don't think you should go tearing back home to Upstate New York on the chance that you might—*might* get a role with Alex Reardon. It's too risky. You're starting to get a name here. People know who you are. . . ."

Cathy's mouth twisted. "Maybe that's a drawback." She lifted her suitcase. "Walk me to the car?"

They went out the door of the second floor apartment. Mrs. Wood's washing fluttered in the breeze in the tiny yard below.

With Cathy clutching her suitcase and Ellen carrying her make-up case, they clattered down the wood steps together.

When Cathy had put her suitcase into the trunk of her dark green Volkswagen and taken back her makeup kit, Ellen caught her elbow. "Has it occurred to you that you might be going from the frying pan into the fire?"

Cathy's violet eyes lifted to Ellen's brown ones. "What are you talking about?"

"Look, I didn't want to say anything, but—well, I'm just so darn worried about you . . ." She took a breath. "Reardon's thirty-five years old and he's never been married. Doesn't that tell you something?"

Cathy's mouth quirked. "It tells me he's single—and maybe a little repulsive. Geniuses often are."

Ellen shook her head, a frown of impatience drawing her fine brows together. "If there's anything he's not, it's repulsive. He's dynamite with women—blows their restraint to shreds—at least he was before his accident. And he's cold and calculating about it. His only concern is the theater. I've heard he doesn't hesitate to make love to a woman in his cast if he thinks she'll work harder because she believes he's in love with her."

"And women fall for that?" Cathy asked, one dark eyebrow lifting.

"He's the kind of man who makes a woman drop into his arms and not care why he's got them open."

Cathy climbed into her little green car and rolled down the window. "Hasn't it occurred to you that I might have developed an immunity to directors?"

Ellen stood silent for a moment, her eyes searching Cathy's face. "I hope you have. I hope you're very immune. I have a feeling you're going to need every single antibody you've got."

She smiled. "Goodbye, Ellen."

"Oh, Cathy," Ellen leaned impulsively forward and grasped her hand, "be careful. Promise me you will."

"You know I'm an excellent driver," Cathy said easily.

"It isn't your driving I'm worried about." Ellen stepped away, her brown eyes eloquent.

With tears in her own eyes, Cathy started the car and headed out toward the freeway. Even though she tried to resist them, Ellen's words played through her mind as mile after mile of road disappeared beneath the stubby hood of her little car. When she stopped in New Mexico that night, the air was hot and dry and the air-conditioning in her room didn't work particularly well. She blamed her inability to sleep on the heat and was glad to get into the car the next morning. Two days later, in Oklahoma she fought her way through a driving rainstorm. Arkansas had a tornado watch. But the vagaries of the weather seemed unreal. What was real were her thoughts, long, endless thoughts of Wade and herself and how things might have been different. But she had to go on and forget her feelings of regret and pain. Her life with Wade was over.

As she neared New York, Ellen's words about Alex Reardon chased through her head in curious profusion. A slight smile curved her lips. Ellen didn't need to worry. Cathy hadn't been a recluse, she had dated occasionally after Wade left her, but she had been careful to keep the relationships light and friendly. She didn't want another romance—not for a very long time—if ever.

She crossed the border into New York. Her spirits lifted and she relaxed her grip on the steering wheel of her Volkswagen. The sky was incredibly blue this morning and the weather warm, just right for the beginning of summer. She had forgotten how dairy country looked with its red barns and black-and-white cattle. There was even a hawk drifting lazily in the sky ahead of her. Fascinated, she watched until the bird floated out of sight.

A car horn blared. She lifted her foot from the accelerator. Tires screeched behind her. Dear God! She was two feet into the passing lane and another car was trying to go around her! She jerked the wheel and shot a panicked glance into the rearview mirror. A large car loomed behind her . . . much too close!

She rammed her foot down on the accelerator. With a wrenching motion, the big car whipped around her. The danger was over and she hadn't lost control or landed in a ditch. But it had been close. Her heart pounded at a furious rate, and she could see the black look the driver of the other car, a man, was throwing her from his rearview mirror.

Reaction washed over her, making her hands slick on the wheel. Her moment of inattention might have killed them both. The cream-colored car moved on, but not before she caught another glimpse of the driver's furious expression as he looked into his mirror to check her position before he accelerated. It was then she noticed he was a fellow Californian by his blue and yellow license plate.

She was sorry she had endangered him. She'd had a close call herself two days ago, and she could guess how he felt right now. She was at fault; she hadn't been paying attention. She had simply been watching the hawk, trying to put herself in its place, trying to think how it would feel to be up there, soaring above the earth. Wade had taught her that. He had opened her eyes, had made her see how skilled acting comes from careful observation. "You look," he had said to her. "You look, but you don't really see . . ." She had been an avid pupil—and Wade had loved that about her. Later, she had learned that was the only thing he had loved. . . .

Her glance dropped to the dash and her lips curved in a smile. She ought to be "looking" at more practical things—like the fuel gauge bumping the empty mark. She would have to stop at the next station.

The moment she drove into the oasis, she saw the cream-colored car. It was parked beside a gasoline pump and the young service attendant was just taking the hose away from the tank. The driver was standing outside his car, his billfold out, ready to pay.

Her nerves jumped at the sight of him. He was tall and lean and disturbingly male, even from a distance. She gave herself a mental upbraiding and dampened that small voice of alarm. How ridiculous! What could he do to harm her? She turned off the car engine and stepped out of the car, telling herself she was letting her imagination run away with her.

The attendant came up to her at once. "Can I help you?" His eyes scanned her slender feminine form clad in lavender silk blouse and khaki skirt and wandered down the length of her long slim legs to her bare ankles before his gaze returned to her face. Though conscious of the sardonic smile that moved the lips of the dark-haired man who stood watching, she remained cool and poised, smiling easily at the younger man. "I'd like it filled with regular, please."

Mentally, she pleaded with the attendant to move aside so she could escape to the snack shop, but blissfully unaware of her anxiety he stood between her car and the gas pump, blocking her way. "You're a long way from home. Can I check the oil for you? You wouldn't want to be stranded on the road somewhere with a burned-out engine."

He'd evidently glanced at her license plate. She longed to tell him that he needn't worry about her, but it wasn't his fault she'd had an unpleasant experience with the man standing stock still on the other side of the pumps, and the attendant's hazel eyes and blond hair reminded her of her brother Cameron so much that she couldn't find it in her to brush him aside with a curt answer. "No," she agreed, "I wouldn't, but as it happens, I had the oil checked yesterday."

He relaxed against the car and looked as if he was settling in for a chat. "You live in California?"

She shook her head. "Not any more."

His eyes widened with delight. "You're moving to New York?"

"It's more a matter of 'coming back' than moving."

"You're from around here, then." Her inquisitor was probably somewhere in his early twenties, not all that much younger than her own age, twenty-six, but she felt light-years older than this boy in every other way. Reluctantly, she admitted, "Yes, I'm from Naples. Now, if you'll excuse me—"

He broke into a broad grin. "My gosh, so am I. I never would have guessed it. Small world, isn't it?" He announced the cliché with fervent enthusiasm of one who has just discovered its truth for the first time and studied her with renewed interest. "You do look awfully familiar." His brows drew together. Then his face brightened. "Cathy Taylor. Judge Taylor's daughter. That's who you are."

Inwardly she groaned.

"I knew your brother Cameron," he went on.

"Oh, really?" she managed, not wanting to encourage him any further.

Cathy made a restless movement and her captor said, "But I shouldn't be keeping you. You're probably anxious to get home and see your family."

"I am rather," she murmured, and watched with relief as he moved towards the back of the car.

"Have you fixed up in no time," he announced. The metallic scrape of the gas cap was music to her ears.

She forced herself to walk with a controlled step to the glass door of the coffee shop but her back seemed to burn—and she knew two pairs of male eyes were watching her.

When she came out into the sunshine minutes later, her dark hair combed, her makeup freshened, and amber sunglasses on the fine bridge of her nose, she felt ready to face the world—or at least the forty-five or so miles of it she had left to drive. She stepped off the curb with her graceful, swinging walk and was thinking only of her eagerness to be back on the road—when she saw him. He was leaning against the door of her car—waiting for her.

Tension curled the inside of her stomach. Despite the warm sunshine, a chill feathered her skin, as if the fine hairs on her arm were standing on end. He wasn't dressed in the vested suit worn by the high-powered studio executives she was accustomed to seeing; his clothes were casual for traveling—cream-colored pants and a short-sleeved dark brown knit shirt. But the sun gleamed off his coal-black hair, and he exuded a virile attraction that made her aware of every inch of him. Those bare arms, crossed over his chest were lean and muscular like the broad chest they rested on. They looked capable of delivering a knock-out punch—or wrapping themselves around a woman with equal devastation. The trim waist was buckled into a leather belt and the strength of his powerful thighs and legs was more than obvious in the light pants. He was relaxing against the side of her car with an easy but dangerous grace. No wonder he handled his car so expertly out on the road! Some wanton corner of her mind whispered that he would handle a woman with the same cool, knowing expertise. The slight mocking smile that lifted the corner of his lips sent a tremor of some unknown emotion through her. He was smiling as if he had read her mind and knew every one of her errant thoughts.

He didn't look as if he had suffered a nervous reaction from their near accident. But even so, she probably did owe him an explanation. Her story would sound slightly crazy to someone who didn't work in the theater—and particularly to this no-nonsense male specimen! She was trying to decide just exactly what she should say—when she looked into his eyes.

They were a curious, glittering green, and they were traveling down the length of her body. She was an actress; she had been looked at often, but not like this! His coolly sexual appraisal made her pulse pound.

Determined not to let him know how much he disconcerted her, she forced herself to stand still and let her eyes drift just as personally over his body. When she finally looked up into his face again, she discovered he was smiling. Fury welled up inside her. All thought of explanation or apology fled. She wanted nothing more than to get in her car and drive away as fast as she could.

As if he read her thoughts, he pushed away from the car and took a step toward her. He walked with a slight—not limp, exactly, but more of a hesitation, as if he had to favor one hip.

She wasn't sorry he was at a disadvantage. She quickened her step and brushed past him, only to find that as she reached to open her door, her arm was caught and she was swung abruptly around to face him.

She had been expecting something—but not this. "Let go of me." Her words were cool and clipped.

"I want to talk to you," he said, in a low and resonant voice that her theatrical ear told her was trained and precisely under his control.

His fingers on her bare arm were pure power, dispensing an electric charge that shot straight through her. She fought the urge to pull away and prayed for someone to come by, anyone, but the place seemed strangely deserted. She was alone with him. "I'm not interested in anything you have to say," she said huskily.

"I'm sure you're not—" he murmured, "but you're going to listen anyway."

Her heart pounding, she said, "Let go of my arm."

He stared at her for a moment and then released his grip slowly. "Don't you think you owe me an apology?"

"I think by now you owe me one." She wanted to turn away—but she couldn't. His eyes held her pinned. He lifted his hand and touched her face just at the crown of her cheekbone. "I'd take better care of that lovely bone structure if I were you—" His fingers were warm, compelling with tangy pleasure, like wine on the tongue. She couldn't move away. "Much better care—" he added as his hand brushed over the bridge of her glasses and down the top of her nose in a dismissive caress that made her unruly body tremble.

She struggled for control. "I'm quite capable of taking care of myself."

"Is your careful driving an example of that ability?"

"Nothing happened. No damage was done—"

His green eyes ran lazily over her body. "Are you quite sure about that?"

Hot color came into her cheeks. She turned away to climb into her car, but he caught her by the shoulder and swung her around again. She was furious and made no attempt to hide it, but she didn't struggle.

A flicker of admiration for her courage flared briefly in his eyes. Then he said, "Tell me you'll try to be more careful in the future."

She fought off his compelling male attraction and lifted her chin defiantly. "Why? Because I frightened you and made you angry?"

A muscle moved in his lean cheek. "Your recklessness isn't confined to your driving, is it?"

She lifted her head and looked boldly into those green eyes that seemed to have dancing yellow lights in them—like the reflection of a fire. He studied her, and it seemed that she could feel the warmth of his fingers through the silk of her blouse. "But recklessness always demands its own price," he said softly. "Sooner . . . or later."

She stared at him for another long moment, her muscles tense with fury. "Let me go." The words were cool and sharp, like shards of glass.

Suddenly he released her. She fought the impulse to run and moved to her car normally. He backed away a step or two, and she closed the car door and shut him out with an intense feeling of relief, thinking how lucky she was that she would never see him again.

He came closer to the car and towards the open window, saying, "At least put your seat belt on."

She realized then that she hadn't been wearing it at the time of their first encounter. "Consider it done," she said, with a mocking bow of her head.

As if her body was against her in every way, her fingers fumbled with the clasp. When at last she succeeded in fastening it, she dug in her purse for her key.

He stepped closer. "Aren't you forgetting something else?"

The dry tone made her raise her eyes to his. "What?"

"You're supposed to pay for the gas before you drive away."

With a little shock, she realized she hadn't paid. But he was the last person in the world she wanted to remind her. His mocking smile and coolly articulated words destroyed the hard-held control she had on her temper. "Your concern is extremely touching."

A dark eyebrow lifted in mocking amusement. "I'm glad you appreciate it. After all, it might prove embarrassing for Judge Taylor to discover that his daughter is wanted by the police."

She made a furious sound in her throat and thrust the door open. The final ignominy was trying to leave the car with her seat belt still fastened securely over her shoulder. His smile of amusement lashed her temper into frustrated fury.

After a short eternity she managed to release the catch, climb out of the car, and walk away from his mocking smile to escape into the air-conditioned coolness of the building.

After she had paid her bill, the station attendant said thoughtfully, "Say, that guy wasn't bothering you, was he? I was watching, but I didn't know for sure if I should step in or not. With both of you carrying California plates," he shrugged, "I thought you might have known him from somewhere else."

She reassured him with a smile. "It wasn't anything I couldn't handle. But thanks anyway." She put the small amount of money she received in change back in her purse. "I'm sure I'll never see him again."

She felt much more confident about the truth of that statement when she stepped out of the building and saw that the cream-colored sedan was gone.

The hot color stayed in her cheeks, even after she entered Highway 15. She followed its curving path south between hills and a lake. She struggled to forget her encounter with that . . . man and concentrate on the way the lake reflected the color of the sky. It struck her suddenly that she had never spent a single complete summer on that lake. She had always been sent to camp—even when she had grown older and expressed a desire to stay home.

Why she had wanted to, she couldn't remember. Her father's house was a cold, dark, and unfriendly dwelling. An avid reader, she used to picture it as in a Gothic novel. It was a house, not a home. A word like *home* held all the connotations of family, closeness and sharing and loving, popcorn popped round a fire-place and roses on the table. Nothing could have been farther from her own home life. The house on the lake was the place where she stopped over briefly to unpack one suitcase and pack another. And now she was going there, hoping to stay all summer, longer than she had ever stayed there in her life . . . and she hadn't even let her father know she was coming.

It wasn't surprising that she hadn't called him. She had not been home in six years, and communication had been sporadic during those years. She received from Melissa, housekeeper and friend, occasional cards, birthday, Christmas, and always an Easter card with extravagant flowers blooming on the front. Otherwise word from home would have been non-existent.

The final break came after her divorce from Wade. When she called her father to inform him of the change in her marital status, he had been chilly and so obviously disapproving that she had concluded the conversation without giving him her new address and the telephone number of the apartment she shared with Ellen.

She wouldn't receive a warm welcome—she knew that. But she knew he wouldn't refuse to let her stay at home. The risk of incurring his momentary ire at finding her on his doorstep and enduring his cool disregard for the rest of the summer could be endured—for the chance to work with Alex Reardon.

There had been many beautiful year-round homes bordering the lake when Cathy was younger—yet to her older, more adult eye, her father's house was still as imposing, still as awe-inspiring as it had been to her as a child. Two-storied white pillars rose to the roof and sheltered the front door. A red-tiled roof gave it the look of a Spanish mansion.

Her stomach churned with anticipation as she reached into the trunk to get her suitcase. She walked up the shallow steps and heard the hollow echo of her high heels on the wooden floor of the portico. Her father would not be home in the middle of a

Friday morning, she remembered with a surge of relief, but it would be good to see Melissa.

She didn't have a key, but she doubted if the door were locked anyway. If she just walked in, she would frighten Melissa to death. She lifted the gold knocker and tapped it against the frame.

The door swung open. An unfamiliar woman stood just inside the entryway. Who was she? The woman appeared to be in her early thirties. Her chestnut hair was pulled back into a neat chignon, and her dress, a pale green silky wrap-around, embodied understated chic.

"Yes?" she said. The cultured voice was polite but cool.

"I—I'm sorry. I was expecting Melissa to answer the door."

"Are you a friend of hers?" The woman's words did not lose their decidedly chilly tone.

"Mom, who is it?" a young girl's voice asked. "Who's at the door?"

The girl who wandered into the hallway behind the woman was an adolescent of perhaps twelve or thirteen. She studied Cathy with the open curiosity of a much younger child.

"I'm not exactly sure, darling," the older woman said, turning to look at the girl. There was a dryness in her voice as she added, "We seem to be at an impasse."

Cathy shook her head. "I think I've made a mistake. I—My father used to live here—"

Color drained from the woman's cheeks. She seemed to stare at Cathy in a stunned silence. Then as if she had recovered slightly, her mouth lifted in a slight smile. "You haven't made a mistake," she said, her voice low and controlled, "Please—won't you come in?" She turned slightly and called, "Melissa!"

Cathy stepped into the hallway and felt as if she had been thrown into a strange new world that was all the more disturbing for its hint of familiarity. The parquet flooring of the hallway under her feet still shone with wax but never in her memory had the dark paneled doors to her left stood open. Now, the doors were gone, and through the open frame the entire room was visible from where she stood. Cream carpeting drew light into every corner. Where depressing brown velvet drapes had hung, cotton curtains the same shade as the carpet lent a feeling of light and airiness. The uncomfortable Victorian sofa had vanished; a low modern sofa curved in front of the fireplace. Inside the grate crimson geraniums in clay pots filled the room with their tangy scent. She could see her own astounded reflection in the mantel-to-ceiling mirror.

Cathy turned. "I would never have believed it possible," she said under her breath. "This room—" she explained to the woman, "It's so different—so comfortable and full of light."

"Why . . . thank you," the woman replied, a faint smile turning up the corners of her mouth. "I think it turned out nicely. I . . ."

"Cathy!" A short woman with sparkling gray eyes stood in the hallway. Melissa too was unfamiliar in a dark uniform and white apron, but the smile she wore and the arms she held out were the same. "I thought my ears were lying. I couldn't believe I was hearing your voice."

"Hello, Melissa." Cathy dropped the suitcase and took the two steps that carried her into Melissa's outstretched arms. "How have you been?"

"I'm fine, love, except I've missed your foolish face." Melissa's greetings never varied throughout the years. They were the one unchanging thing in Cathy's life, the anchor to which she had clung. Once, as a teenager, she had tried to imagine her father hugging her and saying, "I've missed your foolish face," but . . . *stop it,* she told herself fiercely. *That's all behind you.*

Melissa held her away from her. "Drive from the other side of the world, did you? And not a word to the Judge or me about your coming." Her words mock-scolded.

Cathy looked at her, loving the smell of lavender soap that would always mean *Melissa* to her. The housekeeper's eyes were eloquent and the grip on her arms warning, as if the older woman knew her next words would be a surprise. "And you've already met the new Mrs. Taylor."

Only her skill as an actress kept her from gasping aloud. Cathy stared at Melissa. "I—we were just talking about the house."

Melissa released her. "Done wonders with it, hasn't she?" The short woman in the crisp, black uniform stood gazing at the slim figure of the Judge's new wife and Cathy could see that there was respect and liking in that look. Cathy felt a stirring of interest. Melissa's loyalty was not easily won.

Mrs. Taylor seemed to gather herself and remember her role as hostess. "Won't you come into the kitchen and have something cool to drink, Cathy? You must be thirsty after being out on the road."

She desperately needed a moment alone to adjust to the idea of a re-married father. "I'd like to take my things upstairs first—if I may."

"Of course," she said at once. "Your room just needs the dustcovers taken off the furniture and the bed made up—" Mrs. Taylor looked at Melissa, who was already saying, "I'll help you, love—"

"No, Melissa, I can do it. Are the sheets in the linen press?" Melissa nodded. "I'll just be a minute," she said, and picked up her suitcase to turn back to the curving stair.

It was then she heard the girl, who had stood silently at her mother's side say, "But Mom, I thought you said she was married—" A warning *shush* closed off the girl's words, but she felt the heavy silence as two pairs of eyes watched her make her way upstairs.

The winding curve of the steps took her out of their vision. She slid her hand along the smooth wood banister to keep her balance as she carried the heavy case upward. The girl wasn't the only one to be surprised about a changed marital status. She couldn't believe her father, after living for years as a widower, had actually gotten married again! It seemed incredible! She felt a tinge of regret. As a child, she had yearned for a new mother. But now—it was too late.

She went into her room and dropped her suitcase on the stand at the foot of the bed. The pale green rug was soft under her feet as she crossed to the dresser and lifted the dustcover. The dark walnut surface gleamed with the patina of age. Beams of dust danced in the light as she folded the cover and placed it on the floor.

She stared into the beveled mirror of the antique dresser and reached forward to touch the shelf, the empty bare shelf. A tiny black cat made of glass had stood there—until the night she had been so angry she had tossed the cat through the window. Her father had had a man come and replace the window, but he had refused to replace the cat.

That impetuous, hot-tempered child was gone. Now she was an adult.

She took a comb out of her purse and began to run it through her long, dark hair. She had wanted to stay here for the summer and audition for Alex Reardon. But with her father newly married—well, that changed everything. She sighed and laid the comb down. She would have to feel her way carefully, she thought as she started to go downstairs.

The kitchen, too, had been remodeled, and Melissa indicated Cathy should sit down at the high butcher block table that stood like an island in the middle of the room. There were four tall stools around it, and the young girl was already seated in one of them, sipping on a straw plunged into a tall green glass. Melissa placed a similar glass in front of Cathy. Mrs. Taylor poured herself a cup of tea from a teapot on the counter and sat down next to her daughter.

There was a moment of breathless silence, and then Mrs. Taylor raised hazel eyes to Cathy. Her slim hand circled the cup. "I feel I should explain about Jason's silence on our marriage. We—made the decision to marry rather suddenly and then after the honeymoon, when he tried to contact you, he was told you were no longer connected with Metro."

Cathy met the woman's eyes. No, she wasn't working at Metro and hadn't been for six months. She had had to leave the studio to keep from bumping into Wade and his new wife at every turn. "I never thought about my father trying to contact me there."

She shrugged her shoulders slightly, thinking that the relationship she had with her father must seem very strange to his new wife. Cathy wondered what her father had said about her. "Really, please don't apologize. My father and I have gone our own ways for several years. I'm glad for the chance to meet you. When—that is, how long—"

"We've been married two weeks," Mrs. Taylor said. "I had thought we should wait, but—" The woman's cheeks colored slightly. "Jason can be very persuasive when he wants to be—" she said and hastily added, "as I'm sure you know."

"Perhaps not quite in the same way," Cathy murmured and smiled faintly. "And this is your daughter—"

"Danielle. And please call me Audrey."

"Melissa says you're an actress," the young girl said. "What movies have you been in?" Her brown eyes were wide with the beginnings of hero worship, and Cathy thought perhaps Audrey Taylor was relieved to have the conversation lightened by her daughter's questions.

Cathy smiled ruefully. "I was in *Cherish the Woman* and *Tormented,* but you would have to look very hard to see me, I'm afraid."

"Did you see any famous movie stars?"

Cathy named a famous male star she had gotten to know quite well and another petite female star she thought Danielle would know.

"Did you do television?"

"I had a regular job on one of the quiz shows before I was married. I used to smile a lot and wave my hand at all the fabulous prizes the contestant could win."

"Did you like television or the movies better?"

Cathy smiled inwardly at the girl's questions, knowing Danielle was busy imagining herself as a glamorous actress. If only it was as wonderful as people dreamed it was. . . . "Actually, I prefer to work in front of a live audience. Television does have that advantage and of course the money is good. But the theater is my first love. I worked in an off-Broadway show six years ago when I was just starting—and I loved it."

"Mom used to be on Broadway," the girl said.

"Danielle . . ." the woman said sharply.

"Well, it's true," Danielle insisted staunchly. "You've told me about it lots of times."

Cathy's curiosity was aroused. "Were you?"

Audrey smiled. "A long time ago." She looked down at her cup as if seeing something of her past there. Then she lifted her eyes to Cathy's. "I think my career was in the exact same stages as yours when I married Danielle's father. But I believed a woman couldn't be married and have a family and a successful career in the theater too. The stage is too demanding. So I gave up acting to devote myself to my husband and my family." She made an expressive gesture with her slender hand. "Sometimes I've regretted it—especially after Danielle's father died. But—life goes on." She hesitated, as if she were going to say something else—but didn't.

"Mom has a friend from the theater coming here for dinner tonight."

Cathy felt dismayed. She really was intruding. She took a sip of the cool lemonade and tried to think. How could she stretch her meager funds to drive on to New York City—and find a way to finance an apartment and look for a job. . . .

Danielle's voice broke across her thoughts. "Have you ever heard of Alex Reardon?"

The lemonade went to her larynx instantly. She coughed and gasped for air and clutched her napkin to press it over her mouth. Melissa was behind her at once, the uniform rustling as she pounded on Cathy's back. Cathy wasn't sure whether the choking or the flat of Melissa's hand was causing the most distress.

"Melissa, for heaven's sake," she gasped, when she could talk again, "I'm not dying." *Except perhaps from embarrassment.*

"Well, I should hope not," Melissa said with asperity, hiding her concern behind her sharp tongue as she always did. "You haven't choked like that since you were a child."

Cathy wiped away the tears and looked up to see Audrey Taylor half-standing. She had gotten up to—what? Pound on her back with Melissa? Audrey took her seat again, but something flickered in the older woman's eyes, as if she realized Cathy's violent reaction to the lemonade had been in reality a reaction to the name of Alex Reardon.

The woman gazed at her thoughtfully for a few seconds and then said, "You will join us for dinner, won't you? I'm sure you'll find Alex amusing and informative—unless he's terribly changed since his accident."

"He was almost killed, wasn't he, Mom?"

"The doctors didn't think he would live—and then after he regained consciousness, they told him he wouldn't walk again." Audrey looked at Cathy. "But he did. He's completely mobile. The car accident happened three years ago—maybe you heard about it."

"I—I had heard about it, yes," Cathy admitted.

"And did you know he was coming here to Naples to work at his first directing assignment since his enforced retirement from Broadway?"

Cathy nodded and then took a breath. "I—I had hoped to work with him."

"Have you ever met him?"

Cathy shook her head. "I don't think I've ever seen a picture of him, really."

Audrey shook her head. "You won't, either. He's always refused to have anything at all to do with the press and since the accident, he's worse, if that's possible. He's a fanatic about his privacy. It's no wonder, really, a great deal of space was given over to speculation after he was hurt . . . you know the kind. 'Will the brilliant Alex Reardon recover and soar as high as he once did or has he suffered undiscovered brain damage' . . . that sort of thing. Alex has become something of a recluse. I was very pleased when he said he'd come to dinner tonight. I'm sure he'll be interested in talking to you."

"I wouldn't want to intrude—"

"Don't worry about Alex. Believe me, he's well able to take care of himself in any encounter."

"If you're going to be a part of the goings on tonight," Melissa said, turning away from the stove where she had been stirring something hot and bubbly, "you'd better lie down for a while. You certainly don't have a California tan. That pale skin of yours is paler than ever. You look washed out, Catrinka."

Cathy grinned at Melissa. "Thanks for the kind words. You're always so good for my ego."

The woman shook her head. "I mean it. Go make up your bed and get some rest. The world will still be here when you wake up."

Another well-remembered childhood saying. Cathy smiled. "All right, Melissa."

"Dinner will be at eight, Cathy," Audrey murmured.

"I can talk to her more later, can't I, Mom?" Danielle asked her mother anxiously.

"Of course," her mother answered smoothly. "You and Cathy will have lots of time to talk." Audrey looked up and smiled and Cathy thought the woman had comforted her stepdaughter as much as she had assured her daughter—and that she had done it deliberately.

The pale light of dusk filtered through the green curtains. Her eyelids felt like lead weights. She couldn't open them. Somewhere, someone was calling her name. "Cathy, love, are you up and about?"

Cars went down the road endlessly in her brain. Was she still driving? Then she remembered. She was home in her bed, lying between cool, scented sheets, wearing only her underthings. The voice called again. "Cathy!" Melissa was knocking on the door.

She lifted her head and looked at her gold travel clock. Her eyes flew open. Almost seven o'clock! She had slept for nearly five hours.

She tossed back the covers. "I'm up," she said through the door to Melissa, knowing she should be in the kitchen and not up here worrying about her.

"All right, love." Melissa's steps went away from her door and down the stairs.

Cathy switched on the overhead light and looked at herself in the mirror. Her eyes were heavy with sleep and her hair was disheveled. She would have to pull herself together somehow or she would not be a civilized addition to Audrey Taylor's dinner party.

She went into the shower and sluiced water into her face and eyes with her hands cupped to the spray, letting the chilly water wash the sleep away. She shampooed her hair quickly, rinsed it, and got out of the shower. She wrapped herself in a fluffy towel and stepped back into the bedroom. A search through her suitcase unearthed her hand-held dryer. Brushing and drying her hair as she sat on the edge of the bed, she tried to decide what to wear. She had one good dress suitable for tonight, a black silk cut like a slip with spaghetti straps, narrow waist, and a hem that fell in uneven handkerchief points. The creases would fall out of it the minute she put it on. It seemed a safe choice.

Her hair dry, she got into her delicate lace briefs. No bra, the low cut of the gown wouldn't allow it. She slid the silky garment over her head and adjusted the straps on her shoulders. At the mirror she touched her lashes with a mascara wand carefully. She began to think about meeting Alex Reardon, and her hand started to shake. She had to steady it against her chin.

At last satisfied that she had accented the long, full length of her lashes, she applied gray shadow to her eyelids to bring out the violet brilliance of her eyes. Blusher on her cheeks, so her complexion wouldn't look so "washed out," gloss on her lips. She was ready.

She stood back and looked at herself in the mirror. Black dress against creamy white skin, no jewelry. Her coloring was dramatic and she had dressed to make the most of it. Her black hair and white skin had been what had caught Wade's eye. She had thought that was an advantage then. Now—she wasn't so sure. She wanted to impress Alex Reardon—she couldn't deny that. But she had a feeling he was not a man interested in appearances. He might even be prejudiced against her because of the way she looked.

What was he like—this irascible man who bordered on genius? She turned away from the mirror. There was only one way to find out.

She descended the stairs, her heart pounding against her ribs. Her mouth was as dry as if she were stepping out on the stage for the opening night of a play. At the bottom of the stairs, she stood on the parquet floor and took a deep breath, letting it out slowly. Then she arranged her mouth into a smile and stepped into the doorway. She knew the value of an entrance, but she didn't particularly want to pose that way tonight. She was in her father's house. Where was he? She searched for him, and found him standing next to Audrey, one hand around his wife's waist, the other holding a glass he had raised to punctuate a point made to the man standing across from him. She turned slightly, and she could see the backs of the heads of the three people sitting on the couch in front of the fireplace. A woman in pink silk was in profile, laughing at something the man seated next to her had said. . . .

She took a step into the room. At that instant, the man lifted his head. In the mirror that covered the wall from mantel to ceiling, Cathy looked into male eyes that glittered like emeralds in the sun. Shock sizzled through her. It was the man she had met on the road this morning. And with one sharp stab of intuition, she knew that this man was Alex Reardon.

CHAPTER TWO

"Catherine!" Her father's commanding tone stopped all conversation. In that deadly quiet she said, "Hello, Father."

"Come in, come in," her father ordered. "We've been waiting for you."

She unconsciously dug into the poise she had developed as an actress and crossed the room with her graceful walk to step to his side. Steadying herself on his arm, she reached up to kiss him. His cheek was warm against her mouth, his arm iron-hard under her hand. At fifty-two, he adhered to a routine of exercising that gave him the physique of a much younger man. His dark brown suit was impeccable.

Jason Taylor smiled, a movement of his lips that did not reach his eyes. "This is a pleasant surprise. Why didn't you let me know you were coming?" His smooth blandness covered any trace of irritation. "I would have killed the fatted calf."

She gazed up at the face that was already beginning to tan. The silver hair added to his distinguished good looks. "You know I much prefer lobster," she said lightly, a half-smile on her lips. "Save the fatted calf for Cam. How is he, Father?"

"Fine, just fine." Her father's face relaxed into lines of interest and pleasure. She had always considered her father an attractive man, but there was an added glow to his skin and a new sparkle in his eyes. Marriage agreed with him. "Cameron will be home in a few days." Her father paused and then said, "Will you be staying long enough to see him?"

She met his eyes squarely. "I—I really don't know what my

plans are right at the moment, Father." She kept her voice low. The conversational hum around them had begun again, and their words were private. "I don't want to intrude on you and your—wife"

"You won't be," he said, and to her astonishment, he looked slightly disconcerted. "You've met Audrey."

Cathy gave her father a direct look. "Yes, this afternoon."

"Our marriage isn't as sudden as it seems," he began in an uncharacteristic attempt to excuse himself. "We've known each other for years . . ."

She smiled. "Don't spoil it, Father," she said calmly. "I quite enjoyed the thought of you flinging yourself headlong into romance."

Her father looked faintly startled. "You did?"

"Darling, I did want to give you a chance to speak to Cathy in private, but would you mind if I introduce her around now?" Audrey smiled at her husband, and his face immediately softened.

"No, of course not," he said with a smile.

Audrey nodded toward the tall man her father had been speaking to when Cathy came into the room, and the small, blond, fortyish woman beside him. "Cathy, do you know Gerald and Helen Blakely?"

Cathy held out her hand. "Yes, of course. I went to camp with their daughter for several summers. How are you, Mrs. Blakely? And how is Cindy?"

"Nice to see you again, Cathy. Cindy is in Arizona. She is married to a doctor."

"Greet her for me, will you," Cathy said, hoping that Cindy had found the man of her dreams they had talked about late at night in their bunk beds. "How does she like living out west?" She felt a prickle along her backbone—as if the visual heat from male eyes burned into the part of her back that wasn't covered by her gown.

She couldn't have said what the rest of the conversation was about. She was only aware of its end—its inevitable end—and

Audrey touching her arm and saying, "Come, meet the others before we go in."

She was led by Audrey to the couch and introduced to a young lawyer. The man scrambled hastily to his feet and presented his wife, a young woman who was obviously expecting a child. The adoring glance her husband bestowed on his wife as she held her hand out to Cathy made Cathy faintly envious. She had wanted a child—but that was out of the question with Wade.

The flicker of remembrance and regret vanished. Every cell in her body jangled with awareness of the man who had risen from the couch and was leaning against the mantel, his lean body taut in an expensively-cut gray suit, his hair devil-dark.

But in the end, of course, she had to face him. She met those green eyes and something primitive and wild beat in her veins. He looked as virile and attractive as he had that afternoon, more so perhaps. Somehow, surrounded by a civilized setting, there was an elemental vibrance about him that made her nerves tighten in response.

Audrey said brightly, "Cathy, this is Alex Reardon . . . the director."

She tried a light, casual smile, but a backlash of excitement clawed at her throat. She couldn't trust her voice. She extended her hand to him wordlessly, and felt the hard warmth of his on the icy coldness of hers. A hard smile lifted the harsh curve of his lip. To anyone else, she was sure he looked casually polite. "Ms. Taylor." he said.

Her voice, when she found it, surprised her by sounding normal. "Mr. Reardon."

His eyes flickered over her, and then he smiled, as if he were remembering her struggles with the seatbelt. "You reached home safely, I see."

She withdrew her hand from his grasp. "I'm normally a very careful driver, Mr. Reardon. But I—I was sorry about what happened . . ."

Audrey looked at Cathy and drew her brows together in a puzzled frown. "Then you've already met Alex."

"Well—not exactly. That is, we have met, but I didn't know he was—" she faltered, knowing that he would think she was apologizing now because she did know who he was.

"I've already told him about you, Cathy," Audrey said, and inwardly Cathy groaned. "although I don't think I'm doing you a favor, really. Alex is a difficult director to work with. Do you still badger young actresses who happen to fall into your clutches, Alex? Or have you mellowed in your old age?"

It was all said in a teasing tone, and the smile on Alex Reardon's face as he turned toward Audrey was lazily indulgent. "You'll never forgive me for that stint of summer stock we did together, will you?"

Audrey, elegantly dressed in pale green silk, looked far removed from a young girl who might have been shattered by a word from Alex Reardon. Cathy thought they had to be very close in age.

Audrey was smiling. "Did you expect me to? I can't remember disliking anyone quite as much. I plotted your death, you know."

"What did you conjure up for me, Audrey?" came the lazy question. "Boiling in oil? Murder with a dull knife?"

"Something much more dreadful," Audrey said, smiling. "My mind was very devious in those days. Strychnine was a favorite. In my fantasy I put a little in each one of those cups of coffee you drank." She paused for dramatic effect. "Do you think there's a possibility your wine might taste peculiar tonight?"

Alex Reardon turned to Cathy with slow, easy grace. "You're my witness, Ms. Taylor. You heard the Judge's wife say she had a motive."

Audrey said, "Then I must go and ask Melissa to change your wine so I won't be found out. Excuse me, won't you both? I really do have to go and see if dinner is ready."

With a meaningful little smile at Cathy, she drifted away. It was a heaven-sent opportunity. But her brain turned to uncooperative mush, and her throat was dry. She simply couldn't ask Alex Reardon for an audition—not after what had happened this afternoon.

"Audrey's quite something." Alex Reardon stared at Cathy, as if he expected her to make some comment.

"Yes." Cathy agreed, unsure why the intentness of those words made her uneasy.

"She's an old friend," he said, his eyes lazily hooded.

She looked up at him sharply. "Just exactly what is it you're trying to say, Mr. Reardon?"

"Audrey mentioned that you hadn't been home in several years. Seems—strange that you would turn up just now, quit your job and come rushing home after six years of being away."

Cathy stared at him. What was he driving at? Did he honestly believe she was jealous of her father's new wife? Cathy lifted her chin and met his eyes. She knew that all chance of working with him had vanished. "I'm sure you'll be terribly amused—but the reason I came to Naples was to try out for a part in one of your plays."

He stared back at her. "I don't believe you."

She shrugged. "Then don't. It's the truth, whether you believe it or not."

His mouth lifted in a mocking smirk. "I might have—if I didn't know you were born here. With your interest in the theater, you must have known that all the casting for Spring Valley is handled by a committee—and that auditions take place in February and March."

A shock of pain shivered through her. She should have known that—but she didn't. She knew nothing about her home town—or the way in which its regional theater operated. She simply hadn't been here that much. Her look of stunned surprise seemed to puzzle him. He gazed at her. "Is it possible you didn't know?" he asked softly, more of himself than of her.

She shook her head and at that moment, Audrey returned to the room and went to her husband. He announced dinner, and to Cathy's utmost relief, Audrey stepped to Alex's side and took his arm to lead him into the dining room.

All through dinner, she smiled and laughed and gave a reasonable appearance of normality. But inside, her stomach churned.

She was disturbed and upset that Alex Reardon should think her sole purpose for coming to Naples was to cause trouble between her father and Audrey. Why had he judged her so severely after seeing her so briefly? She tried to concentrate on the surroundings, which were elegant. A new chandelier brilliant with crystal pendants hung over the oval table. Light gleamed off the white china, the polished silver. Peach-colored roses floated in a low crystal bowl in the middle of the table.

She ate slowly, savoring Melissa's excellent chicken Cordon Bleu and tried to focus her attention on her father's conversation. He was discussing with the young lawyer who was seated on her left the curious elements of a case he had heard several years ago.

She tried to keep her eyes away from Alex Reardon. He sat next to Audrey on the other side of the table diagonally across from her so he was not directly in her line of vision, but her gaze seemed to drift to him of its own accord. There was a subtle fascination about him in the way the candlelight highlighted the planes of his dark face. One moment the bones were harsh against the skin, the next there were crinkling lines of amusement along his mouth and eyes as he laughed at something Audrey said.

Suddenly he turned his head and looked at her. The mocking curve of his mouth told her it amused him to catch her watching him. She dropped her eyes to her plate at once.

Did he think she still wanted to audition for him? She couldn't, not after what he had said to her. After tonight she hoped she would never see him again.

But when the meal was over, and Audrey invited the guests to go into the living room for coffee, Alex Reardon fell behind the others and grasped Cathy by the elbow. She was too startled to pull away. "Audrey, the meal was delicious," he said blandly. "You won't mind if Ms. Taylor and I skip coffee, will you? I have something I want to discuss with her."

Audrey beamed at him. "No, of course not, Alex. I thought perhaps you'd want some time to chat with Cathy."

There was a soft, intent undertone in his voice as he said, "Yes."

When Audrey had gone, they were alone in the empty dining room. Aware of his masculine attraction with every fiber of her being, Cathy tugged at his arm. "I think we've said all we have to say to each other."

"Shall we go outside?" he said smoothly, ignoring her crisp tone and guiding her toward the sliding glass door.

She could have pulled away from him—but she didn't. Some perverse, wildly excited core of her wanted to follow him into the moonlight. . . .

The drapes billowed inward as he opened the door. Outside, walking beside him across the lawn toward the shore of the lake, the evening air was deliciously cool on her strangely burning skin. The crickets were singing their mating song, and the frogs added their croaking counterpoint. There was a half-moon shining down on the minuscule waves, making them glitter with pinpoints of light.

A familiar moist smell in the air teased her nose as they walked closer to the lake and conflicting emotions rose in her: memories of racing Cam into the water, a new, reckless excitement generated by the man whose hand was on her elbow.

At the shore of the lake, he turned her toward him. His hand fell away from her arm. The moonlight shone down on his hair and made it gleam like black satin—but shadowed his face. She had no idea what thoughts lay behind those dark features. He said, "Have you any ideas about where you'll go—from here?"

His bland tone revealed nothing of his emotions. He'd been a master actor before he turned to directing, she remembered. She wanted to tell him her plans were none of his concern, but instead she shrugged bare shoulders and said, "No."

"I suppose you'll be leaving Naples."

She turned away from him and looked out over the lake. "I suppose I will."

His voice was soft. "I'm—sorry I couldn't have offered you something—"

The easily mouthed platitude made the temper she thought she had learned to control flare into life. She turned to him, her face pale. "You wouldn't have given me a walk-on."

"You think not?" The soft mockery of his tone goaded her like a prod.

"Why don't you just come right out say it? For some reason which I can't possibly imagine you think I'm bent on causing problems for my father and Audrey."

He studied her upturned, pale face clearly illuminated in the moonlight. "Which you can't possibly imagine doing—Mrs. Warren?"

She stared at him, her face white and strained, her eyes brilliant with unshed tears. A low moan escaped her, and she turned to walk away, but he caught her elbow and swung her around to face him. "No, you don't. You're going to listen to the truth, whether you like it or not. Out on the road, your name didn't mean anything to me. But after Audrey told me about your career, I remembered that Wade Warren's marriage had been destroyed by a girl named Cathy Taylor—"

She pulled at her elbow and struggled to get away. She hadn't destroyed Wade's marriage. Wade had argued with her relentlessly until he had convinced her that his marriage was over and nothing could salvage it. Only time had shown that she was right to be wary of him. "What I did or didn't do is not your concern —" His grip tightened. She would have cried out, but she couldn't give him the satisfaction.

"Wade Warren is forty years old—old enough to be your father," he said grimly.

"Wade was older than me, yes. But by fourteen years. He would be delighted to hear how sexually precocious you think he is! Let go of my arm."

"Not until you've heard everything I have to say."

"I don't have to listen to you—"

"Do you deny you married a man old enough to be your father?"

"What business is it of yours?"

His words were low and warning. "Stay away from Audrey."

His determination to protect her father's wife made her feel empty—and alone. "Believe it or not," she said coldly, "I like Audrey very much. I hope she stays with my father forever. I have no intention of doing anything that would jeopardize her happiness."

His eyes searched her moon-illuminated face. His fingers loosened.

"Now, let go of me, Mr. Reardon."

He tightened his grip on her bare elbow. "No," he murmured softly, "not just yet." His dark head lowered, shielding her from the moonlight. An almost intolerable excitement robbed her of the will to move. His mouth came down slowly, slowly toward hers. When she thought she could no longer bear the waiting, he took her lips with a warm tenderness and a male possessiveness that made her heart rocket in her breast. She tried not to respond, but she felt herself weakening, kissing him back hungrily, sliding her arms up over the smooth fabric of his jacket.

Abruptly, he pulled away, and she felt only an exquisite sense of loss.

There was a long, eloquent silence before he murmured, "So a man doesn't have to be two decades older than you are to turn you on."

She stared up at him, feeling the blood drain away from her face. "Were you conducting an experiment?"

"You might say that," he drawled.

Anger consumed her. "Oh, leave me alone," she cried out in anguish and whirled to escape when his hand clamped around her wrist. He pulled her around to face him with a quick, hard movement.

"Where are you going?"

"Anywhere," she said huskily, "anywhere, as long as it's away from you—"

Inexorably, he drew her close and locked her inside his arms again. "An experiment can't be considered valid unless the results are repeatable . . ."

"Damn you!" she shot back at him, her eyes purple with fury. "I'm not a laboratory specimen—"

He moved swiftly, taking her lips with masterful sureness. She had betrayed herself too much; he was confident in his ability to arouse her now, and though she fought to keep her mouth cool and placid, he touched the upper curve of her lip with his tongue as if he knew exactly how sensitive she was there, and her tiny gasp parted her lips enough to allow him entry. His hands tightened at her back and waist and hips, sending feverish electric charges through her wherever his fingers pressed, and his tongue claimed her mouth, probed and discovered with a thoroughness that made desire bubble up in her like an artesian well. He was taking, and she was giving, in an embrace that was nearly as intimate as that last final possession.

Someone laughed up at the house and the sound brought a flood of cool reason to her brain. She put her palms against his chest and pushed. He released her at once.

She stared up at his dark face. His expression was hidden from her in the dark. She sighed softly and turned away.

"Cathy, wait. Listen—"

She had listened too long. She ran up the lawn, her heart pounding, her mind reeling with a deep sense of self-disgust, shutting the sound of him calling her name out of her mind. She couldn't listen to any more of his hateful psychoanalysis of her character. He was wrong—wrong! He had accused her of breaking up Wade's marriage . . . Dear God, how unfair that was! She hadn't destroyed Wade's marriage. She would have had to have been a fool not to have noticed that his eyes were on her constantly during that first movie they made together, but she had rebuffed Wade again and again when she learned he already had a wife . . . until the day he convinced her that his marriage was over . . . and that he genuinely cared for her—and wanted to marry her. In the end, it had been she who had convinced him age didn't matter. Her youth had bothered Wade, but it hadn't stopped him from making love to her. And once she had lain in his arms, she could not envision life without him.

Yet their marriage had ended in less than a year. Wade had wanted to make her his Pygmalion, mold her in the image of what he thought she should be. He had wanted to make her career decisions. She had balked—carefully at first—then with more and more determination. When she turned down a movie part he had wanted her to accept, Wade had simply walked out of her life. The divorce papers came quickly after that and a year later, he had remarried a woman younger than she—and infinitely more malleable.

She avoided the living room and quickly climbed the stairs. Was it possible Alex Reardon was right—that she had been attracted to Wade simply because he was so much older?

No, her mind cried, *no.* She had dated many younger men before she married Wade.

In her room she went to the window and looked out over the town. Old-fashioned street lights gleamed in the summer darkness. If she left Naples, she would be admitting that Alex Reardon was right about her. She couldn't do that. She had fought for the right to live her own life—both with her father—and with Wade. She couldn't—wouldn't—toss that away after one skirmish with Alex Reardon. Then too, her funds were very low. To go to New York City was the logical thing to do, but the trip and the deposit on an apartment would completely deplete her bank account. And she would still have to look for a temporary job of some sort to support herself until she managed to find something in the theater.

She was foolish even to consider it. She couldn't leave Naples. She couldn't afford it—either financially—or emotionally. But could she afford to stay?

A fierce resolution hardened inside her. *Let Alex Reardon think whatever he wanted to think!*

Then, in the quiet of the room that had been hers as a child, an overwhelming depression swept over her. She lay down on the bed and stared blankly at the ceiling, knowing that she would not soon forget the way he had held her in his arms—and kissed her.

CHAPTER THREE

"You can go right on in." Patty Brown held open the door to James Carson's office and her voice was friendly, but Cathy could see the curiosity in her blue eyes. All of Naples must know she was job hunting, Cathy thought ruefully.

She rose to her feet and tugged at the navy skirt of her suit. "Thanks, Patty." James was the fourth lawyer she had seen that day. She had felt a little strange seeking out the lawyers she had met at her father's house—but sometimes they had extra typing, transcripts they needed of court testimony or legal papers to be typed immediately. She was well able to do that.

Patty led her into an office that had the atmosphere of a lawyer who had begun to practice about the same year as Lincoln. Dust motes danced in the air in a light stream from the window. Ancient books lined the walls from floor to ceiling. James sat behind the broad surface of an oak desk littered with papers. "Well, this is a surprise," he said, rising and indicating she should sit in the chair next to his desk. "How are you, Cathy?"

"Fine, James." She smiled and settled into the chair. James was the antithesis of her father and in some ways he looked older—even though he was only a few years her senior. The blue sweater he wore over his white shirt was worn at the elbows.

"Are you here on legal business?" he asked.

"In a way," she said, wondering what she should say and in the end deciding that the simple truth was best. "I'm looking for a job."

He sat looking at her quietly. Lawyers were a patient breed—

she knew that. She was related to one—and soon it would be two, when Cameron finished his schooling. This one hadn't batted an eyelash. The chair creaked under his weight as he teetered back and studied her. "Why?"

She hadn't expected that—but she should have. "Why does anyone need a job?" she asked lightly.

He sat, coolly complacent, his eyes fastened on her. "Your father is a wealthy man."

She kept the smile on her face. "But I am not a wealthy woman."

"You mean you can do secretarial work?"

"Yes. Most people in the field of acting have something else to fall back on. They have to," she said lightly.

He shook his head. "I'm sorry, Cathy. I don't have enough work to keep Peggy busy."

She felt the color come to her cheeks. "I see. I'm sorry—that I put you on the spot—" She stood up, feeling sick and ashamed, but he was out of the chair and at her side before she reached the door. "Cathy. I wish I could help you, I really do." He gazed down at her. She had forgotten how massive his shoulders were. She vaguely remembered something about his being a football star for the local team. "Why did you come to Naples?" he said, his eyes quizzical. "New York City is where you should be anyway, where there are opportunities for acting."

She nodded. "Yes, I know."

"Then why did you come back here?"

She tried to smile. "It—it was something that didn't work out." She lifted her head. "Well, thank you for your time anyway, James." She left him standing by the door with that faint, quizzical smile on his face as she tossed a quick good-bye over her shoulder to Peggy and went out.

The stairway was dark and cool. Each tread creaked a protest under her high-heeled shoes. At the bottom, she opened the door and stepped out into the sunshine, pausing for a moment to let her eyes adjust before bending her head to look in her purse for her ignition key. Her fingers closed around it. She brought it up from the depths of her bag and raised her head—just in time to see that she was on a collision course with a woman hidden behind a brown bag of groceries.

She tried to stop, but she couldn't. At the impact, the bag broke. Lettuce, carrots, and a tin can of coffee bounced to the sidewalk, and Cathy found herself gazing into the perplexed face of a plump, elderly woman.

Color crept into Cathy's cheeks as she knelt to the scattered groceries. "I'm terribly sorry," she said, picking up the articles and replacing them in the torn bag as best she could. "I should have been watching where I was going. . . ." She handed the bag to the woman and looked beyond her shoulder . . . straight into the sardonic face of Alex Reardon.

"That's quite all right, dearie," the woman said cheerfully, taking the bag and adjusting it in her arms for safer carrying. "I haven't lived to be this old without surviving a bump or two. But I'd watch my step a little more if I were you." The woman nodded sagely, stepped around Cathy and walked away.

"My sentiments, exactly," Alex drawled.

The hot color flared again, and she moved to brush past him.

He caught her arm. "Where are you going?"

His tone was casual, maddeningly so. Why was it he was so little affected by the encounters that set every nerve she had on edge? "To my car."

"I'd like to talk to you a moment."

Another woman walked by and glanced at them curiously. "I think I've heard all I care to hear of whatever you may have to say to me." She wrenched free of his grasp.

"Cathy."

Why did his voice command obedience without question? "Yes?"

He held up his left hand. The key chain that Ellen had given her with its two sterling silver masks of tragedy and comedy dangled from his finger. His eyes on her face, he slowly and deliberately pocketed it. As if he read every moment of her inner struggle to control her temper, he said softly, "I want to talk to you, and I don't want to conduct the conversation on Main Street."

He stepped forward, grasped her elbow and shepherded her down the street to his car. "Get in," he said softly.

She hesitated. Other than tackle him physically, there was little she could do but play along with him. She knew she was insane to expose herself to the double danger of his sexual magnetism and his antagonism, but there was nothing else she could do.

He headed out of town and down the winding road that skirted the lake. "What are you doing out so early in the morning?"

"Nothing of importance," she lied.

He was silent for a moment. Then he let his eyes travel over the tailored navy jacket and suit skirt, down her nyloned legs to the closed-toe pumps on her feet. "Right off—I'd say you were job hunting."

She looked away from him out the window and didn't answer.

"I owe you an apology," he said quietly, startling her, "or if not an apology, at least an explanation."

"You don't owe me anything," she said coolly.

He gave her a shrewd side-long glance. "Then you've forgiven me for my ill-tempered remarks of the other evening?"

She was silent. He wasn't apologizing for kissing her. Had those moments meant anything to him at all? Before she could arrange her thoughts and give a suitable reply, he said softly, "You see? You haven't, have you? Give me a chance to explain. Say you'll have lunch with me."

He had caught her neatly. The silence grew. She floundered for something to say, failed, took a breath, swallowed, and tried to ignore the attractive look of his face mottled by patterns of sunshine and shadow as they rode along. He looked younger, more vibrant, and disturbingly attractive, if that was possible, than when she last saw him. As if he sensed her resistance weakening, he smiled and said in a soft, persuasive voice, "I've been working eighteen hours a day for the last three days—and it suddenly occurs to me that I deserve a few hours off. Spend them with me."

Working long hours must agree with him. He looked more rested than he had three days ago, more—approachable. Could she disguise her awareness of him for a short length of time? It would be difficult—but not impossible. And why shouldn't she accept his invitation to lunch? He was holding out the olive branch. What possible harm would there be in declaring a truce with Alex Reardon? "All right," she said huskily.

"Where are we going?" she asked. "I don't remember a dining place out this way."

He smiled. "Don't you?"

He pulled the car easily into the parking lot of a redwood A-frame house nestled down against a hill. He helped her out of the car and down the path. When he had unlocked the door and she stepped inside, she gazed around, entranced. "It's beautiful," she breathed.

The entire west wall was glass, giving a clear view of the lake. A free-standing black enamel fireplace stood in the corner with a pipe that soared to the ceiling. In front of the fireplace lay a black fur rug. Behind the rug was a long sofa upholstered in a plush cream velvet. The house was casual on the surface—but full of texture and variety and subtle surprise—like its tenant.

Alex walked past the snack bar that divided the kitchen from the living room. "Sit down," he said easily, moving to the bright yellow refrigerator, and indicating a stool on the other side of the snack bar. "I'll have things ready in a minute."

"We're eating here?" she asked, intrigued.

"No," he said, taking out bowls and arranging them on the counter, emptying their contents on a round cutting board. He reached for the handle of a knife that was anchored in a wooden block, pulled it out and began slicing vegetables using short, quick strokes, his other hand on the tip of the knife.

"You look very professional doing that," she said.

"What do you think I did to support myself while I was a struggling actor?" One dark eyebrow arched at her in mock amusement. "I couldn't type." The mental picture of him seated at a typewriter made her suppress a smile. He saw the quirk of her lips. "Watch it, Ms. Taylor. Your chauvinist attitude is showing. I know some very capable secretaries—who happen to be men."

To distract him, she said, "Did you work as a cook—really?"

He looked pained. "I was not a *cook,* I was a master chef in an Oriental restaurant famed for its dinners prepared and served before your very eyes, madam." A dip of his head simulated a bow.

She smiled. His answering smile brought a warmth to her cheeks that he didn't see, for just then he bent to pull a wooden picnic basket out from under the counter and began to systematically fill it with food, plates, and flatware. When he finished, he handed her a low, flat pan with a cord. "You take the wok. I'll bring the basket and the wine."

"Where are we going?"

He pointed past her shoulder. "That way."

Flushing with pleasure, she picked up the wok and followed him out of the house, across the wooden patio and down the four concrete steps to the dock. Her high-heels clicked on the wood as they walked toward the end. She knew by now that he planned to travel by boat to their destination, wherever it might be. She wasn't really dressed for a boatride, but the powerboat that sat cradled in the hoist next to the dock was elegant enough to have accommodated a party dressed in evening clothes. A gold metallic color on the outside, the inside was posh with lush brown carpeting and leather bucket seats.

He reached up and unlocked the ratchet on the wheel of the hoist. The boat swayed down and settled into the water. "Here, give me that," he said, taking the *wok* from her hand. "Take hold of my arm and climb in."

The warm, bare feel of his flesh under her fingers was disturbing—but she couldn't take her hand away. She did need his support for stepping in her high heels from the dock—which was solid—to the boat, which was rocking gently in the water. She climbed in, her narrow skirt riding up her nyloned thigh. Inside the boat, she turned, just in time to see a gleam in his green eyes that was quickly hidden behind dark lashes. He handed her the wok and the basket, then swung down easily into the boat beside her. A key was inserted in the ignition, and instantly there was a low growl of response from the engine. When they had cleared the dock, a burst of speed carried them away from land toward the center of the lake.

"We must be going to Roseland." The amusement park at the other end of the lake was bordered by a picnic ground that was accessible from the water.

He only smiled and eased the throttle forward. The boat surged with a force that threw her against the back of the seat.

She sat back and began to enjoy the beauty of the day. She was protected from any spray by the high windshield. The sun was warm on her top of her head and she seemed to be submerged in blue: blue sky, blue water. Crystal clear and spring-fed, the lake was translucent in the deep center. She stared out over the water and had time, too, to contemplate the change in Alex Reardon. His skin was a light tan, and there was a decided air of something about him she couldn't describe—a lighter, happier state of mind—as if he had wondered whether he could resume work in the theater—and discovered that he could. She was mentally listing all the things he would have had to have done since arriving in Naples: get acquainted with the cast, start blocking the action, discuss costumes with a volunteer designer, begin set construction—when his dark hand eased the throttle back and they began to slow down. By now, they were squarely in the middle of the lake, but because it was so narrow the surrounding hills weren't more than a mile away. She looked at him quizzically. He idled the boat to a full stop and then killed the engine . . . and dropped the anchor.

She had, for a few moments, forgotten that subtle attraction, that male virility that drew her like a moth to the flame. But now, in the sudden quiet and subjected to his darkly penetrating gaze, it flooded her with renewed intensity. She moved nervously under his scrutiny.

He asked softly, "Is something wrong?"

"No," her voice caught on a breathless husky note as she told the lie, "not at all. I just hadn't expected to be eating . . . on the boat."

"Would you rather not?" He studied her and at the shake of her head reached for the wok. She handed it to him, trying to ignore the firm leanness of his hand and the tiny black curling hairs on his arm.

"No—no, it's perfectly all right." She added her spoken approval to her gestured one. But it wasn't all right. There were other pleasure craft cruising in the blue waters and several sailboats drifted by them, true, but they were very much alone . . . together.

He got up from his seat and went to the back of the boat where he plugged the wok into an outlet. She fought to keep her eyes away from him rather than turning to watch him prepare their food. In the end she lost the battle, and her eyes followed him and wouldn't be torn away. He was a master at movement. She was sure he would catch and rivet any audience's attention—no matter what he was doing.

After the wok had heated, he emptied the chopped carrots, celery, zucchini and shrimp into it. The muscles of his arms moved as he swirled the food around in the hot pan and a teasing aroma of hot spices reached her nose. When he had finished, he divided the food equally between two plates and brought out a loaf of bread which he cut and sliced. "Come back here and sit. It's easier to eat," he invited her.

She hesitated and then stood up to move back to the opposite side of the impromptu table. He produced a bottle of wine, opened it, and poured it into glasses he had packed in the basket.

"What shall we drink to, Cathy?"

His voice had deepened. Her mouth seemed to go dry. She fought the urge to moisten her lips. "To the success of *Cactus Flower,*" she said coolly, and raised her lips to the glass.

For a silent, heart-pounding moment his eyes met hers over the rim of the glass. "I wouldn't think you'd be much interested in the success of my plays—after what I said—"

"It's not the first time I've been condemned on circumstantial evidence." No longer able to meet the probing gaze of his eyes, she tilted her head and drank. The dry, tart taste of the wine flowed into her mouth and tingled on her tongue.

When she placed the glass carefully back on the table, she knew she should never have come out with him. Her pulses pounded, her skin felt hot—and its heat had nothing to do with the warmth of the sun. That same sun shone on the dark silk of his hair and gleamed off his skin. She could see the fine dark hairs that nestled in the hollow of his throat, the way his arms moved when he lifted a morsel of food to his mouth. She tried to concentrate on her own food; it was crispy and delicious, but her appetite was gone. She reached for her wine, and just then, another powerboat sped by. She smothered a startled gasp and barely avoided spilling the wine into her lap.

"Careful," Alex warned. "Did you get any on your skirt?"

She shook her head and set the glass back down. "No. No damage done."

He looked pointedly at her hardly touched plate. "My cooking isn't to your taste?"

"No, really," she assured him, "—it's—excellent, delicious. You're a marvelous cook—chef." She was stammering like a child. She had to stop this ridiculous schoolgirl reaction to Alex Reardon. She wasn't a schoolgirl, she was a mature woman. But the uniqueness of eating in a boat on the lake took on a new significance. She couldn't just get up and walk away from him.

A breeze touched a lock of his hair and blew it over his forehead. He thrust it back impatiently. "Cathy, I want to apologize for the other night." He paused and gazed at her. "I'd been thinking about my own problems all that day and I wasn't in the best frame of mind. I know that isn't a good excuse, but . . ."

"Please," she said huskily. "I—it doesn't matter." She forced her eyes away from him to look out over the water. "You weren't the first person to accuse me of marrying Wade for all the wrong reasons. I don't suppose you'll be the last."

His next words were soft and intent. "Why did you marry him?"

Her soft rueful laugh floated out over the water. "I married Wade Warren because I loved him—or thought I did."

"And now?"

She turned to give him a direct look. "Would you mind very much if we talked about something else?"

His brows drew together in a frown, but his voice was coolly polite. "I'll get these things put away and we'll start back. Would you like to move up front out of the way?"

He was quiet as he put the food and wine back into the basket, pulled up the anchor, and got the boat under way. But when they had traversed the lake and come to a halt beside the dock, he helped her out of the boat and then said in a noncommittal voice, "We'll carry this stuff inside first. Then I want to talk to you."

Inside the house, he stowed the food away as quickly and efficiently as he cooked. "Sit down," he said to her, gesturing at the sofa. "I'll only be a minute."

She settled into the couch, focusing her attention on a wooden carving of a duck that sat in gleaming elegance on the coffee table. It was a wild duck, its wings spread, the bird just on the verge of lifting into flight. Graceful and evocative, it stirred her deeply. She wondered if it had been a gift to him after his highly successful direction of Ibsen's play *The Wild Duck*.

He came out of the kitchen and settled himself on the other end of the couch. There was a width of a cushion between them.

He sat for a moment and then turned slightly, bending his knee and lifting his arm to lay it along the back of the low sofa. His fingertips were very close to her shoulder. "It's occurred to me that we could solve both our problems at the same time," he said softly.

She raised an eyebrow. "Oh?"

"You need a job—and I need an assistant."

"An assistant?"

He traced a finger idly over the velvet material of the couch. "The day I got here, I got word from my assistant that he had had a job offer from a theatre in the South—and that he was accepting it. I was—angry. I knew I was in no frame of mind to attend Audrey's dinner party. I wanted to stay home and swim myself out of my rage—but I also knew how disappointed she'd be if I didn't show up. And I have to admit—I was—curious to see you again."

She fought the husky tone with anger. "You had the advantage. You knew who I was."

"Yes—" he said slowly. "I thought I did. I thought I knew your type well. The spoiled little girl with the rich father—who had married an even richer husband." He hurried on, as if to take the sting from his words. It didn't.

"Then Audrey mentioned some of the work you've done, the plays you've been in. Your credits are impressive."

"I'm glad you're impressed, Mr. Reardon," she said in a cool tone.

He made a gesture with his hand. "I'm going about this all wrong. What I meant to say is, if you're forced to stay in Naples all summer, then you might as well be working in the theater rather than pounding the keys of a typewriter for some lawyer who wants everything done in triplicate."

"Seven copies is standard," she said, her voice dry. "I'm sorry, Mr. Reardon. I'm an actress, not a director. I know nothing about your field."

He smiled. "All the better. You won't be tempted to tell me what to do." He seemed to tense the muscles of his body slightly, as if he were trying to focus all his physical energy on the task of convincing her. "Look, I really do need your help. I don't have the time to advertise and interview a dozen people in order to find someone suitable. And you've had enough experience in the theater to know your way around without my holding your hand." He paused, and then added, "Don't think it's a glamorous job—it isn't. In fact—the first thing I'll ask you to do is type the cast roster. I was tearing my hair out with that this morning—and it was the reason I was in Naples. I was looking for someone who types at home to do it for me.

"But in addition to the menial jobs—you'd broaden your concept of the play. You would be seeing a production from a broader viewpoint—the wide-angle lens—the view of the director instead of the smaller focus of an actress. Will you consider it?"

She was tempted—dear God, she was tempted. But—

He seemed to sense her indecision and to press his advantage said quickly, "You'll learn about set design, costuming, lighting, scheduling rehearsals, working with people. And the money is good. Not great, but good." He mentioned a figure far beyond anything she could have earned as a part-time secretary.

But . . . there was this ridiculous attraction she felt toward him. How could she combat that, seeing him day after day? Yet it was a perfect solution—a way to stay in Naples, earn some money, and work in the theatre. If only . . . the chime of the doorbell interrupted her thoughts.

Alex's face was dark with annoyance, but he rose lazily to his feet.

The voice at the door was low and musical and feminine. "Hello, darling. Umm, you look about twenty-one in those jeans. Kiss me."

After a silence that indicated Alex must have complied with the request, the voice went on, "This house is terrific. How on earth did you find it? And here I am living in that dreadful guest place with a chatty old lady right out of Ibsen. Wouldn't you like to have a roommate?"

That well-modulated, trained voice was directly behind her and Cathy turned. She had seen Pamela Field on television and once in regional theatre in Los Angeles but up close, the stage vivaciousness that characterized the well-known actress's appearances seemed to border on brittle tension. The effort to project an image of youth was heightened by the silver star she had pinned on the side of her blond hair. She was not as tall as she had seemed on the stage, but perhaps that was because she was wearing flat sandals with her white shorts and halter top. She dropped the string bag she was carrying on one of the chairs and Cathy could see a silky suit and towel inside.

"Pam, this is Cathy Taylor." Imperceptibly, Alex moved away from the immaculately groomed hand that lingered on his arm.

"It's nice to meet you, Ms. Field." Pamela Field's hand had been familiar and possessive—the caress of a lover. She remembered now that there had been much speculation in the press about Pamela and Alex after the accident. The story was that they had been lovers and that Pamela's interest in Alex had evaporated after he was injured.

"Are you in the cast?" Pamela asked.

Alex answered for her. "I've just asked Cathy to be my assistant."

Pamela smiled up into his face. "And did she say yes?"

"She's thinking about it."

Pamela Field's long-lashed eyes turned back to Cathy. "Smart girl. I'd give it careful thought, if I were you." She walked to the couch and sat down. Her voice had a touch of earnestness, artfully mixed with a mocking, teasing tone. "Alex demands perfection—" one delicate blond eyebrow arched as Pamela smiled at Alex, "and he's a perfect devil to work with."

Alex leaned lazily back on a stool beside the snack bar, and rested one white canvas-shod foot on the rung. His smile mocked her faintly. "I can't recall being particularly hard on you in the last few days."

"That's because I've learned a few things in the years since I worked with you." She ran a long, red fingernail along the tufted crease in the back of the cream velvet couch. "I've learned that you need me as much as I need you."

"You're not—irreplaceable, Pam." There was a heavy quiet in the room. Pamela Field raised her head to stare at Alex, her face colored with displeasure.

Cathy dug her nails into her palms and wished she were

somewhere else. There was an undercurrent of tension in both Alex's and Pamela's words that made her positive they weren't talking about the play. But if they were at odds, Cathy was sure it was only temporary. They had been lovers—and obviously were again.

To make matters worse, she couldn't get up and leave. Her own car was on the main street of Naples—and the ignition key was in his pocket.

"You know, darling, you did promise me a boat ride," Pamela said, her color subsiding.

Quickly, Cathy stood up. "I really should be going—" and looked at Alex.

He straightened from his perch on the stool. "Pam, I have to run Cathy back into town."

Pamela Field smiled. "That's all right, darling. I'll catch some sun while you're gone. Will it be all right if I run upstairs and change?" Her bright smile made it clear that she expected his nodding assent. Pamela rose and turned to Cathy. "It was nice to meet you. Perhaps we'll run into each other again soon."

"You'll be seeing a lot of her as my assistant," Alex said assertively.

"Will I?" Pamela murmured.

Cathy got up from the couch and walked past Pamela. Alex took her elbow, his fingers hard and compelling on her arm.

It was warm in the car. He switched on the air conditioning and they rode to Naples in a heavy silence that was broken only by the sound of the cooling machinery. When they reached the town, heat waves radiated from the street. No one was out in the brilliant sunshine.

She opened the door and got out of the car. Alex unfolded himself from under the wheel and walked lazily around the side of his car to stand looking down at her. One hand slid into the pocket of his jeans. He brought out her key, but he didn't move to hand it to her. "May I have your decision by tomorrow?" His face was cool and remote.

She nodded.

"Call me before noon." His eyes held hers as his fingers brushed her palm to lay the cold metal in it. "I'll be at the theater after that."

"All right."

His hand lingered against her palm. "Thank you for having lunch with me." His voice had that quiet, intense quality she was beginning to know well.

With an intense exertion of her will power, she lowered her hand away from his and closed her fingers around the key. "I—enjoyed it very much." Her voice came out low and on the verge of huskiness. She turned away. Sliding into her car, she thrust the key in the ignition. The engine turned over immediately. She pulled out into the street, her mind in a disturbed state. Something compelled her to glance into her rearview mirror as she drove away. She lifted her eyes—and her nerves leapt. He had not moved. He was standing in the middle of the street, watching her. She averted her eyes from the reflection of his lean, male figure and gave the accelerator a savage push.

That night, she undressed and lay down in bed, her state of mind just as disturbed as it had been that afternoon. She lay in the dark and let the truth she had tried to subjugate float to the surface of her mind. She was attracted to him. There, she had admitted the truth to herself at last. Could she work for him without giving herself away? She turned over, trying to get comfortable. She was an actress—and if there was one thing she had learned in the months that had followed Wade's rejection, it was how to hide her emotions. But . . . did she dare risk subjecting herself to a daily dose of Reardon charm? He did have charm. She would never forget their afternoon on the lake. She raised herself on her elbow and punched the pillow. Perhaps she would be able to think more clearly when the afternoon she had spent with Alex faded into the mists of her mind.

She slept reasonably well, and in the morning the sunlight that blazed into her room made her thoughts seem clearer. She was foolish to turn down Alex's offer. After all, she had driven the length of the country on the chance that she might be offered a bit part under his direction. Instead, he was handing her the opportunity to sit beside him for the entire summer and absorb as much of his technique as she could. She would be exposed to more new ideas in nine weeks than she had been in the last two years—since Wade went out of her life.

What difference did her personal feelings make, really? After those punishing kisses beside the lake, he hadn't touched her. And since that night . . . he and Pamela seemed to have resumed their love affair. Or if they hadn't, it wouldn't be long before they did, if Pamela had her way. The thought jarred—when it should have comforted.

With a sudden determination she threw the covers back and got out of bed. She showered and dressed in a pair of faded denims and a T-shirt. Her purse held the notebook that contained Alex's number. She found it, and with a light, quick step she bounded down the stairs to the hall telephone. She dialed his number and as it rang in her ear, turned to lean against the bannister. She was humming to herself tunelessly, waiting impatiently for Alex to answer at the other end—when she looked up and caught sight of herself in the huge mirror above the living room fireplace. She hardly recognized herself. Her cheeks were flushed and there was a glitter of excitement in her eyes that hadn't been there for a very long time.

"Hello?" Alex's voice deepened the color in her face. Without any conscious thought, she snatched the phone away from her ear and cradled it, hanging up quickly.

She stood still and lifted cold hands to her cheeks. It was no use. She couldn't work with Alex day after day and hide the emotions that made her light up inside like an incandescent lamp! Anyone as observant as Alex would notice her emotional turmoil at once.

If only she hadn't spent that afternoon with him. She would not have gotten into the boat if she hadn't believed they were going to Roseland, loud, noisy . . . safe Roseland.

The amusement park. She could look there for work. Cindy Blake had worked there one summer when her parents thought she was too old to go to camp. Perhaps she could find something there too. At least it was another place to look. Then, if she didn't find anything . . . she would know she had exhausted every possibility before she gave in and called Alex.

A small voice inside her head whispered that she should leave Naples and not look back. She ignored it, picked up her purse, and hurried out of the house.

CHAPTER FOUR

The manager of the amusement park shook his head. "Sorry. We've got teen age kids from all over the area applying months ahead for work here.

Moments later, grateful to be out in the sunshine away from the odor of his cigar, she stood for a moment, trying to decide what to do. From across the street, a car, a dark sedan with a dented fender, drove by and honked. The driver stuck his head out the window. "Hello, Cathy."

It was James. He smiled, and his friendly smile was welcome after the brusqueness of the other man. He said, "What are you doing in Canandaigua?"

She gave him a rueful smile. "Job hunting."

Some undefinable emotion crossed his face. Then he said, "I have another errand, but how about if I pick you up for lunch? Meet me back here at twelve?"

The thought of sharing a lunch with James was far too appealing to reject. Still, she said, flicking a hand down her denims, "I'm not really dressed to go out."

He was unperturbed. "We'll go somewhere suitable."

She smiled. "All right, fine then."

"Good." He grinned and looked pleased. "I'll see you later."

Not knowing what to tell Alex, she put off making the telephone call till a few minutes before noon. By then it was too late. He didn't answer the repeated ring of the phone. She didn't know whether to be relieved or disappointed.

When she climbed into the car beside James, his smile helped lessen her anxiety. He began to talk easily, telling her about the part for his boat he had driven to the marina to purchase. She found his company soothing after her difficult morning. She sat back and relaxed, the tails of the yellow scarf she had wound around her hair fluttering in the breeze from the open car window. How relaxing it was to be with him. She would have a pleasant lunch and forget Alex Reardon, forget that she would have to accept his offer.

She did have a pleasant lunch with James, far too pleasant, she thought as she finished eating and leaned back in her chair. He had taken her to a place on the lake that only the local people seemed to know; there was little possibility she would encounter Alex here. The thought added to her relaxed state of mind. They sat at a round, umbrella-shaded table on a deck built out over the water. At one side of the platform, weeping willow trees swayed and on the other, cottonwood tree leaves rustled with a papery rustle. The breeze feathered over her skin and lifted the tails of her scarf. She fingered the stem of her glass, a small sigh escaping her lips.

James smiled. "Glad you came?"

"I had forgotten about this place. It's peaceful, isn't it?"

He nodded his agreement.

"Sometimes I think the Finger Lakes are the most beautiful in the world," she said, her eyes lifting to the water. "Is that why you stay here?"

"Yes. I couldn't leave. But—if you love it, too—why did you go away?"

She shook her head and gave a half-laugh. "I wanted to be an actress."

His face serious, he asked, "Then why did you come back? Because of Reardon?"

She gave a short, quick nod. "I had hoped to get a part in one of his plays."

"And he refused to audition you?"

"All the parts are cast."

James rubbed his chin thoughtfully. "Yes, I suppose they are.

The try-outs were months ago. But sometimes people decide to quit—"

"No one has." She looked at him quizzically. "How did you know about the try-outs?"

"I'm in this summer's production."

"What part are you playing?"

"Julian Winston."

Her eyebrows shot up. "James! I didn't know you were interested in the theatre. You must be very good."

"I've had some experience—I guess that was what convinced the committee to give me the chance. I've appeared in every play they've had since I came back from law school. Most of the parts were smaller, though."

"I'm impressed. You're very lucky to be working with Alex Reardon." Her lips twitched. "You'll probably learn new techniques to improve your courtroom presentations."

"I already have." He put his hand over hers. "Cathy. Reardon needs an assistant. Why don't you apply for the job?"

"I—he had asked me but—"

"But what?" His eyebrows raised slightly.

"I—" she hedged, not wanting to discuss her personal life with him, "I wasn't sure I wanted the job. When I decided I—did, I wasn't able to get in touch with him—"

James shook his head. "That's right. He and Pamela were going around this afternoon to talk to the backers and personally invite them to the dinner dance. It's a time-consuming job. The cast offered to split the list with him, but he refused. I half-expected the two of them to turn up here for lunch. Nickolas has contributed a sizeable sum to the summer's productions."

Her voice still casual, her mind avoiding the topic of Alex Reardon, she said, "I wonder why Nickolas would be so interested in the theatre."

James smiled. "His Greek blood, probably. They say Reardon has Greek blood in his background, too." He glanced around again. "I was mistaken about their itinerary, I guess. I was sure Alex mentioned that they would be here for lunch."

Her pulse pounding, she managed to say in a teasing voice, "Were you hoping to see your leading lady, James?"

He chuckled. "She's about a thousand miles out of my league. At any rate, she's not interested."

She ached to ask why he thought so, but she knew she didn't want to hear his answer. "Why haven't you ever gotten married, James?"

"I am married," he said calmly.

An unpleasant little shock sang through her nerves. "I thought you knew," he said softly.

"No . . . no, I didn't."

With a wry glance, he said flatly, "It isn't what you're thinking. We're separated. She's in New York, trying to break into show business. We met in the Community Theater. Ironic, isn't it?"

She nodded, not knowing quite what to say.

"I suppose a divorce is in the cards eventually." His voice was even. "But right now she keeps me as a sort of safety net to fall back on—I think."

"You must love her very much."

He gazed out over the shimmering blue of the water. "I suppose I do. I only know I can't leave here—and I can't let her go."

Impulsively, she put a hand on his arm. "I'm sorry, James. I know how you must feel. I—hope things work out for you."

He turned and looked at her, his eyes eloquent, his hand capturing hers. "I didn't ask you out to listen to my troubles." He caught her hand between both of his and brought it to his mouth. "But I appreciate your kind words." He brushed her fingers lightly with his lips.

It was the click of high heels against the redwood deck that first warned them they were not alone. But some sixth sense, a prickling at the back of her neck told her the exact identity of the owner of those shoes—and the firm male tread beside them.

James released her hand reluctantly and murmured, "Now I'd call that a badly timed entrance."

She looked up at the couple walking toward them, and her

only coherent thought was that Alex's face would have made a stone mask look lively.

To James, Pamela said, "Nickolas told us you were here." The silver star had been replaced by a gold one that glittered in the blond tresses. Pamela looked alluring as usual, in a green halter dress that left her shoulders bare. As she walked beside Alex, patches of enticing creamy skin were visible on the sides of her body. At their table, she turned to look out over the lake. "What a gorgeous view. You were right about this place, darling." Tilting her head gracefully, she smiled at James. "Are you just finished or may we join you?"

"We are finished but—" James rose and pulled out a chair at the table. "Why don't you sit down? We can stay for a few minutes more. How was your morning?"

"Busy." Pamela settled into the chair James had pulled out for her and Alex stretched his lean frame into the one beside her. His eyes played over Cathy and there was a sardonic twist to his mouth that sent a little chill of fear over her skin.

"Alex has been dragging me around to see dozens of people, dangling the promise of lunch in front of my nose to keep me going." She leaned back in the chair. "I'm exhausted."

"How did you make out? Are all the backers coming to the dance?" James asked.

Pamela sighed. "Of course. One elderly woman is panting for a chance to dance with Alex, isn't she, darling?" Pamela flashed a smile up into his darkly impassive face.

"Is she?" he drawled. "I wasn't aware that I was the answer to her maiden's prayer."

Pamela laughed, a low, throaty sound. "Then you didn't see her looking at you with those lusty eyes." She linked her arm through Alex's and turned her face up toward his. "I can tell her right now she can look all she wants—but she mustn't touch."

"I don't imagine I'd fall apart at a woman's touch," was the dry rejoinder.

Pamela laughed and said something to James that Cathy didn't catch. The actress went on talking to James, and Cathy found her eyes wouldn't leave Alex's face. He moved slightly, and the navy blue shirt he was wearing seemed to intensify the dark sheen of his hair. His eyes met hers. She glanced away, the sharp tingle of nerves making her clench her hands in her lap. No, he wouldn't fall apart at a woman's touch. But an intolerable sense of excitement rose up within her at the thought of touching him, holding him. . . . Deliberately, she used a technique she had learned in theater school to make her mind blank and cool. She nearly succeeded—when Alex cast a mocking glance over her and said softly under the cover of Pamela's words, "I can see why I didn't hear from you."

His eyes flickered to James and then back to her. She stiffened with annoyance. "I tried to call you a few minutes before noon. . . ."

His eyes gleamed. "Are you going to take the job?"

She nodded, her throat full.

"We aren't having rehearsal tonight, but I'll pick you up about six Monday evening." The words were carelessly said, as if he had little interest in her affirmative answer.

She made an effort to match his coolness with her own. "I'll be ready."

Monday evening, she got into the car beside him, her heart pounding with anticipation. Even in the soft light, she saw something flash in his eyes when he looked at her. But he said nothing, and after they had driven to the theater and gone inside, she forgot her nerves as he handed her a note pad and rehearsal began with a minimum of fuss.

As the play progressed, there were little things that her practiced eye noted—the careful balance of the figures on stage, the way movements and words seemed to work as integrated parts of the character portrayals, the way each member of the cast related to the others onstage and gave their performance that spark of reality.

She found she was able to write down the things Alex told her with ease. Her own experience in the theatre made his observations quite clear.

Alex ended the rehearsal promptly at eleven o'clock. Before she could hand the note pad to him and ask him to skim her handwriting to see if anything in it was unclear, he was out of his seat and walking toward the stage. One by one the cast called good night to each other and left the theater, but up on the stage Alex caught the arm of a young, red-haired girl and began speaking in a low tone to her. Cathy stood up with her note pad in her hand, thinking she might as well leave the pad on the seat and go outside—when Alex's voice came across the stage. "Wait a minute, Cathy. I want to talk to you." He turned his attention back to the red-haired girl and his words came across the empty theater to Cathy's ears. "Think about it, Barbara. Remember even though she is a funny little idiot, Toni cares about people."

"I'll try to remember, Mr. Reardon."

"Think back on the times you've felt like Toni. I know you're newly married and your emotions are not those of a girl who's in love with a married man. But think about the times you've struggled to do something in the right way—and it turned out all wrong. Toni's like that. She's a heroic figure battling against the odds life has thrown her. That's the admirable thing about her. She's impulsive and crazy—but still trying to do the 'right thing.' "

"Yes—yes, I see."

The dark head nodded. "Think about it. Try to absorb her through your skin."

"I will, Mr. Reardon."

"That's all, Barbara. I'll see you tomorrow."

"Yes. Good night." The red-haired girl picked up her purse and adjusted it over her shoulder—with a distinct sense of relief, Cathy thought, as she watched the other girl walk up the aisle. She understood how Barbara felt. Even with her own experience in the theater, Alex's quick and intelligent character analysis was rather frightening.

Her own need to escape the quiet of the theater and Alex's

presence made her raise her voice and call to him, "Did you want to look this over before I go?"

He didn't answer. Instead, he stood on the stage and stared across the empty seats at her—making her senses pulse with awareness of him and their aloneness in the darkened theater.

"Come here." His voice was crisp and cool.

She gripped the pad. "I beg your pardon?"

"Come here—up on stage." The command was repeated with the same cool authority.

Her brain screamed danger. She clutched the pad of paper and slanted her body to step out from between the seats. Her feet carried her down the aisle, while her nerves quivered with apprehension. He stared at her till she thought he must know exactly how every muscle in her body worked. She halted at the bottom of the steps. "What did you want?"

"I want you up here."

"It's late and I—"

He came to her, grasped her hand and pulling her forward, and her own electric reaction to his hand made her stumble on the second step. He caught her. Defensively she held the pad of paper between them, but he seized it and tossed it to the floor. He pulled her to center stage, the grip on her hand hard. "Audrey told me you were the understudy for Michelle Landis in *Destiny's Children.*"

She managed to nod, her apprehension growing.

He faced her. "Do you still remember the climactic scene—the one where the woman finally admits to the man that she loves him?"

"Yes," she said, her voice low.

Very softly, he murmured, "I want you to audition for me with that scene. I'll play the part of the man." Ignoring her dazed, stricken look, he commanded, "Start just as she makes her final entrance. She says something like 'I didn't expect to find you here.' "

" 'I didn't think I'd find you here' " she repeated automatically, correcting him, stalling, trying desperately to think of a way to avoid doing that explosive romantic scene with him.

He picked up the line as if she had thrown it to him for a cue and said the next one. " 'Where did you think I'd be?' "

Mesmerized, unable to stop herself, she answered with dialogue. " 'With Gloria.' " The action called for her to turn her back to Alex and she did it with a sense of relief. " 'You belong with her—you told me that.' " Too late, she remembered that Alex was supposed to seize her shoulders from behind. She steeled herself for the feel of his hands on her body. He gripped her, and the leap of reaction from her skin to his fingertips devastated her. " 'Yes, I told you that," he said harshly, in character, " '—to get some kind of reaction out of you. But it didn't work, did it? You escaped—pride and heart intact."

His voice was soft and goading and utterly in character, but something about the words made them seem as if they were directed at her personally. Her response was primitive and yet channeled through the words of the playwright. She whirled around under his hands as the script directed and looked up into his face. " 'Why shouldn't my heart be intact? You've never touched it.' " She increased the emotional intensity in her tone. " 'You gave me expensive gifts—but nothing of yourself. Were the diamonds and rubies and pearls supposed to be a substitute for the love I needed?' " She paused to give her voice the irony the next line called for. " 'Or did you merely want me to feel—grateful?' "

" 'I didn't expect gratitude.' "

Her voice was thick with the restrained emotion the part demanded. " 'Then what do you want from me?' "

His eyes played over her face. " 'The simple admission that you love me.' "

" 'Your calling that . . . simple—shows how little you understand me.' "

How seductively soft his next line! " 'I understand you—exactly.' "

She lifted her head and her eyes glittered with both her acting skill and her emotional reaction to the man who stood holding her. " 'You don't. You don't understand the first thing about me—' "

The script called for her to be pulled into his arms and kissed fiercely and Alex didn't hesitate. He grasped her and pulled her close to him and his mouth came down on hers, hard and punishing. She thrust her hands between them and struggled as the script directed, the unconscious part of her brain registering the cool firmness of his mouth on hers, the warm scent of his body, the lovely feel of his hard flesh under her hands . . . and then she was engaged in a desperate battle to keep from relaxing into his arms and returning his kiss with an urgent need of her own.

He lifted his mouth and said, " 'Admit it. Admit you need me—' "

"All right.' " Her voice trembled and rose gradually as she said the next line under an emotional strain that had little to do with acting. " 'I need you, want you, love you. Does that satisfy you?' " She lifted her head and tried to radiate the pride she thought the character must feel. " 'But what I want and need doesn't make a damn bit of difference to you, does it? And I can't take that any more. I'm leaving you, Joss,' " her voice throbbed with hurt and anger and pain, " 'and I won't look back.' "

Alex released her and she straightened and walked off right as the script directed, leaving him on the stage alone.

The theater was utterly quiet. She heard him say in a low tone, "Cathy, come out here."

For a long moment, she clenched her hands, the nails biting into her palms. She was burning up inside, superheated from the charge of the emotions she had created—and the ones she hadn't. But she forced herself to walk back out onstage.

His gaze was fastened on her, his mouth hard. "You must know how talented you are."

She struggled to contain the anger and frustration that welled up inside her. He had kissed her—but it meant nothing to him. He thought only of her talent. He was telling her she was good, and she should have been ecstatic. Instead, she felt a dull, throbbing ache inside. "I've studied under some excellent teachers," she told him.

"If circumstances were different—I'd recommend that you go to New York immediately. I have a producer friend who could help you. . . ."

His voice trailed away and she stood watching him, fighting the conflicting emotions that warred inside her. "You said—if circumstances were different."

He gave her a bland look. "Right now, I'm not interested in furthering your career."

She gritted her teeth and then said, "Because you need me here."

He nodded. Her voice husky, she said, "Is there a possibility you might give me a recommendation at the end of the summer?"

His voice was soft and cool. "That rather depends on how the summer goes, I think." He turned away and walked down the stairs. She stood stock still, fighting to regain the control of the hot temper that had been easy to contain—until the day she met Alex Reardon.

CHAPTER FIVE

She had been working for Alex almost two weeks—when Barbara Stanton walked in late to rehearsal.

"We've been waiting for you, Barbara." Alex's words were soft—but his voice carried to the farthest corner of the theatre.

"I know, Mr. Reardon, and I'm sorry." The girl reached the stairs, climbed them, and turned to face him, brushing a strand of bright red hair away from her face in an unconsciously defensive gesture. "It—won't happen again."

Pamela had been doing a scene with Devlin Smith, the young man playing Igor, but they both lapsed out of character and gazed out into the dark at Alex. The theater was deadly quiet.

Sitting next to him in the fifth row, Cathy shifted her legs and pushed the yellow legal pad to a less precarious place on her knee. Her restless movement made her elbow brush Alex's on the armrest they shared and he turned his head. She met his gaze steadily. He stared at her and then turned back to the stage. In the light spill, his profile seemed that of a stone mask. "The rules were clearly outlined the first night. One more time and you'll be replaced."

Barbara lifted her head and stared out into the darkness, her eyes bright in the spotlight. She had a clear, translucent complexion and at this moment, her skin was suffused with color. "I'm sorry," she repeated. "It was—unavoidable."

Alex made no reply—but neither did he tell Pamela and Devlin to begin the scene again. He slumped in the seat and directed his gaze somewhere over Barbara Stanton's head.

He was angry. No one moved or spoke in the silence. She waited for the explosion, but the quiet continued, and then she knew that she had been subconsciously expecting Warren's pyrotechnics. Alex Reardon's style was far removed from Warren's yelling and arm-waving. Alex was in control of himself, and because of his superb self-discipline, he was in control of the cast. Blocking went smoothly the first week, and during the next week of interpretation, he made his suggestions with tact and consideration. He treated Pamela exactly the way he treated the rest of the cast with one exception—he did not read Pamela's lines to her. He didn't hesitate to read a line to the less experienced actor or actress, but with Pamela, he took time to discuss the feeling and the motivation behind that feeling. Cathy knew Pamela would have resented line-reading immensely—as she herself would have.

Alex broke the silence. "Let's get started." A sound like a sigh of relief went through the theater.

He straightened and fastened his attention on the stage. They were trying to get an unbroken run-through of one complete scene. Pamela began to speak, and Alex's mouth thinned. In a low tone he said, "Remind me to tell Pam about that line. She's supposed to be prim, not provocative. Carson's leaning against the desk again—*Señor* Sanchez needs more brashness—"

She wrote furiously. At least her experience in the theater kept her from asking Alex to repeat or explain some of the terms he used.

Promptly at eleven, Alex stopped the rehearsal. After the cast left and they were alone in the theatre, he turned to Cathy. "There are a few more things I want to get down. Smith's eyes never seem to be in the right place. Why does he have the peculiar habit of looking away from people just before he delivers a line?" He slanted a look at Cathy. "It can't be because he's shy."

Devlin Smith was a good-looking young man, and he had sought Cathy out during every break. She shrugged. "He's developed the habit of looking away, I suppose," she said carefully.

Alex pushed himself up out of the plush seat. Cathy rose too and walked behind him to the stage. It was their night for cleanup.
"He is very good-looking." Her voice was casual as she unplugged the coffee pot and started to lift the heavy urn off the table.

"Don't pick it up." He held a battered saucepan under the spigot and turned the handle. Steaming black coffee poured out. "His type appeals to women." He paused and then drawled, "Hot and handsome."

She didn't answer. She wasn't going to be drawn into an argument with him about Devlin Smith. Instead, she bent to retrieve a paper cup that had fallen to the floor. She tossed it in the wastebasket—and straightened just as he did, meeting the full force of his eyes. She fought to keep her eyes on his while a peculiar silence hung in the air.

A smile suddenly twisted the corners of his mouth, and he pivoted away, carrying the saucepan of liquid.

She knew he would have to go behind the stage to the dressing room to drain the pan into a sink. His absence made her muscles sag in relief. Alone on the stage, she emptied the coffee grounds into the wastebasket and tried not to think about her own reaction to Alex Reardon. She was familiar with the magnetism and presence an experienced actor could project at will. She knew how devastating such a man could be.

She put the cap on the powdered cream substitute and used a paper towel to wipe up the table. Alex returned, and carried away the coffeepot, and in minutes their tasks were completed and they were walking out of the theater together.

She had fallen into the habit of riding to rehearsal with Alex. The very first night of her job, after all those miles of driving across the country, her car had refused to start. She had discovered the next day that it was a simple matter of putting water in the battery, but Alex had insisted on continuing to pick her up and take her home because, he said, her riding with him gave him the opportunity to discuss problems both before and after rehearsals.

Now, however, as he turned the car and drove out of the parking lot, he was strangely silent. The theater was dark, a shadowy peaked form under the late night moon. Hills covered with grapevines surrounded them as they drove. The sky was blue-black, the stars close and bright.

Desperately, she turned her mind over for something to say. Her wit had deserted her. She could think of nothing but the fact that they were together in the car and that she was sitting on the leather seat beside his hard, male body with no barrier between them. She was immune to directors, she told herself fiercely. She had to be! One heart-wrenching relationship with the breed was enough.

They were on the curving lake road now. The trees that had made light and shade play over his face that day they lunched together now filtered moonlight over his dark features. She turned away to look out into the soft, warm night, but even though she could no longer see him, every cell of her body was still aware of him. His harshly attractive profile seemed imprinted on her brain.

He pulled into the circular driveway behind the stubby little Fiat that gleamed silver gray in the moonlight.

"Your father has a visitor."

She shook her head. "No. That's Cam's car. He's home from school," she said, feeling suddenly lighthearted at thought of seeing her brother again.

"Cam?" His voice held a note of something more than just simple curiosity.

"My brother, Cameron." She found the door handle. It felt cool under the warmth of her hand. "Good night, Mr. Reardon."

His hand grasped her arm. "I'd like to talk to you for a minute."

Instinctively, she sat back in the seat, hoping that those warm fingers would release her if she complied at once. They lingered on her bare arm and were then withdrawn. "Yes?" She wanted him to say what he had to say. She wanted to get out of the car, to run away from what she was feeling, what she was thinking.

"You thought I was too hard on Barbara."

For a moment she couldn't think of what he was talking about. Then she remembered. He must have sensed her thoughts exactly when he sat there with her in the darkened theater. She must remember that and not make the mistake of thinking him insensitive. "I'm not a director, Mr. Reardon." Her voice had an odd, husky quality that almost betrayed her.

Perhaps it did betray her. His hand found her wrist. "Stop calling me that!" he ordered her sharply. "You make me feel like a grand old man of the theater. I have a first name. Use it."

"If that's . . . what you prefer," she said coolly, fighting to control the finely tuned humming of her nerves at his caressing touch. And there was no other word for that movement of his hand on her. He was caressing her wrist in the most sensitive spot—just where the vein pulsed close to the surface.

"I also prefer honesty." Each word was spaced like the tiny flick of a whip, but his fingers continued their provocative movement over her skin giving her a sweet, exquisite pain. She tried to ease her wrist away—and his fingers tightened. A surge of excitement and anger and fear made her lift her head. "All right," she said huskily. "Yes. I think you were too hard on Barbara. The girl carries something with her into rehearsal—some—burden. It takes her awhile to forget whatever it is that is bothering her and drop into the character of Toni. When she does relax—she's very good. But she is struggling with something. You—added to her struggle tonight."

"An astute observation," he said thoughtfully. "Would it surprise you to know that I was aware of Barbara's difficulties?"

She twisted in the seat slightly to face him, longing to tear her hand away from his grasp. But if she did—she would be bringing to their attention what they both—by some tacit understanding—were ignoring. "Yes, it surprises me. If you knew—why were you horrible to her in front of the others?"

A dark eyebrow lifted. "Was I—horrible?" His actor's skill

gave the word an inflection that imitated her tone exactly. "I thought I was the soul of restraint."

"You must know the effect you can exert if you care to," she said coolly.

"I wasn't aware that I had any special 'effect' on people," he said softly. His thumb rubbed lightly over her wristbone. There was a silence in the car that seemed to reverberate in her ears. Then he said softly, "Do I—have an effect on you?"

She tried a subtle sliding movement of her hand to escape his grip, but his fingers tightened. "I don't know what you're talking about . . ."

"Don't you," he murmured.

With infinite slowness, he tightened his grip on her wrist and drew her closer. She was powerless to move or protest. Every particle of her knew what was going to happen—and wanted his kiss. Her other hand came up instinctively to lay against his chest on the soft material of his knit shirt. "Alex—"

She felt the sudden, swift shudder that passed through his body at her husky whisper of his name. Then, without warning, his mouth swooped and took hers. Warm and male and possessive, his lips tenderly learned the shape and form of hers. His hands slid down her back over her T-shirt along the length of her spine, and she had a sudden intense need to feel his fingers on her naked skin, to know the imprint of his hand on her flesh. He lifted his mouth and his warm breath filled hers. "Cathy."

The tantalizing nearness of his mouth made her lean against him and offer her lips to him again. He didn't refuse. He took the sweetness she offered him quickly, touching her lips with his tongue, and when she relaxed, her lips parting under his, he probed her mouth with a tenderness that sent aching need tingling to the bottom of her spine. His hands on her back pressed her closer, crushing the softness of her breasts against his chest.

He lifted his lips—but he did not let her go. His hand on the back of her neck pressed her head against his chest. How good it felt to be in his arms, how right and real! Then suddenly, surprisingly, he released her. She was free.

She turned toward the door with an intolerable ache of rejection when his soft voice stopped her.

"Cathy."

"Yes?" Her voice was husky and disturbed; he was silent as if he were assessing the depth of her disturbance.

"I'll try to be more careful with Barbara in the future." Before she could reply, he asked, "Will you be home tomorrow afternoon?"

She turned back, but he had moved slightly so that his face was shadowed in the corner of the car. She couldn't see his expression. "I suppose so—why?"

"I may have some work for you," he said. And then, in cool dismissal, "Good night, Cathy."

She slid out of the car and shut the door. Almost at once he reversed the gears and was backing around Cam's car and in seconds, he was gone.

She walked into the house, feeling shaken and confused. She saw the light flickering into the hallway from the den, and she knew that her father and Cameron were talking. If only . . . she had someone to talk to. She hesitated in the hall. But long experience at trying to talk to her father made her turn and climb the stairs.

A drop of water hit her face and then another, and another. She opened her eyes cautiously and saw Cameron leaning over her with a cupped fist, the water glistening on his knuckles. She pushed his hand away and sat up. "You haven't indulged in that trick since you were twelve," she drawled.

He smiled, knowing she wasn't really upset. "I'm regressing to childhood," he retorted, hazel eyes laughing at her. He was dressed casually in a pair of faded jeans and a T-shirt that had shrunk in the wash. His blond hair gleamed in the sun. He sat down on the bed to look at her. "How are you, sister dear?"

"Tired. Must you get up with the birds? Good grief, that sun is bright. Pull the shade, would you?"

"Nothing doing. Rise and shine, Cath. We're going water skiing, and I need you to watch."

She rubbed her eyes and tried to bring his face into focus. "Must you be so bright and coherent at this time of day? How can I watch when I can't get my eyes open?" She lay down, turned her back to him, and covered her head with the bedclothes.

"Cath, I'm warning you," Cameron said, tugging at the blanket. "If you don't get up, I'm going to call out the reserves to deal with you."

"Call out the whole militia if you like. But leave quietly, will you please? I'm going back to sleep."

"Cathy, you're my only hope." He was plainly begging. "Audrey and Danielle went into the city with Dad."

She sighed and closed her eyes. "All right, Cam. Just let me sleep a few more minutes . . ." She relaxed, knowing why she was so tired. Each rehearsal seemed to drain her of energy—and after last night . . . If only she hadn't gone into his arms so eagerly! She couldn't let that happen again. She had to stop riding to rehearsals with him. But if she did, he would know at once that the kiss had meant more to her than it had to him. And even if she no longer rode with him, she would still be in constant contact with him for hours every day. How could she hide the fact that admiration for his directing technique and an appreciation for his talent was intensifying her awareness of him as a man? After last night, he must know she wasn't indifferent to him. Would he want an affair? And there was Pamela. . . .

She heard Cameron's footsteps going down the stairs. It was uncharacteristic of him to go away before she actually got out of bed. She snuggled into the warm cocoon of the covers. How did Cameron think he would go skiing? Their boat was still in storage, she remembered, before she drifted back to sleep.

Something wet splashed on her face. She moaned and squeezed her eyes tighter. "Be a good little preppy and go away. I'm sleeping."

Something light brushed her temple. She put up her hand to

fend off another attack from Cam—and knew the minute her fingers touched his face that it was not Cam who was leaning over her. She opened her eyes—to find she was looking directly into Alex Reardon's.

"What are you doing here?" Angry and disturbed, she sat up in bed and hitched the covers around her shoulders, but not before she saw his eyes flicker over the creamy skin under the lavender straps of her gown.

Coolly, he stood and studied her, a slight smile lifting his lips. "Your brother thought I might have better results waking you up than he did." His eyes gleamed. "He was right, it seems."

He bent and sat down next to her on the bed. Her heart rushed up to the base of her throat and started beating in a heavy, slow rhythm that made breathing difficult. He let his green eyes make a lazy tour of her bare face and tousled hair, and she could feel the quick warming of her blood in her veins. "What are you doing here?"

"I was—curious."

"About what?"

"I wanted to see what you look like before your shield is in place."

"I don't know what you're talking about." She bent her knees to hug them to her, effectively disguising the shape of her body under the covers. "What do you want?"

He lifted one dark eyebrow. "Do you really want to know?" he teased, and she felt her cheeks warm.

Absurd though it was with him seated on her bed, she tried to affect a businesslike manner. "You had mentioned dropping by in the afternoon and I assumed you had work for me to do."

He glanced at the gold travel clock beside her bed and his mouth quivered. "It's nearly afternoon now. Don't you think you should be getting up?"

She stared at him. Not a trace of self-consciousness flickered in his face. He looked quite accustomed to sitting on the edge of a woman's bed. Perhaps he was. His skin glowed and his body was lazily relaxed. Had he spent the night with Pamela? The thought made her stomach lurch. "I will get up—when you leave."

His lazy gaze traveled over her face. "I'm supposed to stay until you're on your feet."

"Believe me, I'm wide awake," she shot back defiantly. She had never been more so. The blood raced around her body in warm awareness.

He moved slightly on the bed, and the light blue T-shirt and faded jeans molded to his lean hips emphasized his masculinity. "I believe you are." He glanced at her clock again. "You have exactly ten minutes. If you aren't downstairs by then," that dark eyebrow rose, "I'll come up and put you into the shower . . . personally."

Her voice low, she said, "No."

He raised his finger and traced a circular path on her shoulder bone. "Yes," he murmured, "and with great pleasure."

She stared back at him. His cool green eyes took another tour of her bare shoulders. Male appreciation shone in his eyes and he made no attempt to hide it. The nerves under the bone he was touching seemed to explode.

"I could teach you to enjoy being in the shower with me," he murmured. The words were light and mocking, but there was an undertone of seriousness that made her nerves quiver. Then the dark lashes came down over his eyes. Before she realized what he was doing, he grasped her shoulders, brought her close to his chest and took her mouth with a cool expertise that was utterly devastating.

When she felt as if his kiss was grasping at her very soul, he lifted his head and smiled down into her face. "You now have nine minutes to dress," he said softly. He leaned forward and touched her lips once more, lightly this time, his mouth just brushing hers. Before she could move or protest, he got to his feet and walked out of the room.

He was gone—and she was left with a confused mingling of relief and disappointment. She threw the covers back and got out of bed. Her skin was warm with feverish excitement. In five minutes, Alex Reardon had aroused her out of sleep—and created a fierce need in her she didn't dare think about. She went into the bathroom, stripped out of her nightgown and turned on the shower with a sudden savage twist, flicking it over to cold.

Out of the shower, she pulled on her black maillot over her slim hips, tied the strings at her hips and neck, and covered it with jeans and a sleeveless bit of black silk that knotted under her breasts at her midriff, vowing to herself that she wouldn't let him near her again.

She walked down the stairs and went into the kitchen. Her eyes flew to Alex. He was laughing, head thrown back, body shaking, his whole being given to enjoyment, one lean leg anchored on a rung of the high stool across from Cam. For a moment, she couldn't drag her eyes away. Then she crossed to the cabinet and pulled a heavy pottery mug from the shelf with hands that shook, poured herself a cup of coffee and sat down on the same side of the table as Cam. She lifted the warm coffee cup to her lips and met Alex's eyes. He wasn't laughing now, but laughter still lurked there, along with something she couldn't—didn't dare—name.

He glanced down at his watch. "Seven minutes and forty-two seconds. Not bad."

Cam grinned. "I told you she'd get out of bed for her boss."

"Yes," Alex murmured, and the reverse innuendo gleamed in his eyes like a little flame.

Color flowed into her cheeks. If Cameron noticed the loaded silence, he pretended not to and said, "There's eggs and bacon in the oven, Cath. Some of Melissa's pecan muffins, too."

She slid down from the stool, picked up the potholder, and took the warmed plate with the muffins out of the oven. A hot, fragrant smell filled her nose. Melissa's mother had given her the muffin recipe and they were a favorite of both Cam's and hers. At the table she took a muffin to her plate, cut it and buttered it—feeling Alex's eyes on her every minute.

"Have one, Alex," Cam urged, taking the holder and sliding

the warm plate in his direction. "They're really good—Melissa's specialty."

She watched with fascination as a long, lean-fingered hand plucked a muffin from the plate. Alex copied her movements, slicing and buttering the hot roll. He put a morsel in his mouth. "Delicious." But he was looking straight at her.

She picked up her coffee cup and sipped from it, using it as a shield to ward off his eyes—and distract her from her own thoughts. In the sunlit kitchen, Alex was as leanly attractive and magnetically male as he had been in her bedroom, and the memory of those intimate moments lingered inside her head. Cam went on talking, luckily, and she tried to present a blasé appearance. She ate her muffin and drank her coffee and shut her eyes to the husky, attractive sound of Alex's voice as he replied to Cameron's questions. As a result, she hadn't the remotest idea about what they were discussing, and in the end, when Cam said, "Is that all right with you, Cathy," she could only look at him blankly.

"Haven't you been listening?" Cam chided impatiently. "Alex has offered to take me water skiing—if you'll observe."

She glanced at Alex and something in his eyes made her look away. But she would be safe enough from her own errant thoughts with Cam along. . . . "I—I suppose I can."

When they finished eating, Alex walked out to the dock toward the boat and Cam disappeared into the garage. She lingered behind, waiting for Cam. When he reappeared carrying the blue Fiberglas skis, she said to him in a low tone, "How did you meet him?"

Cam shrugged. "I was out on the patio when he cruised by. He docked, came in, stuck out his hand and told me who he was. We talked for a while, and a trick water skier came by. I said I'd like to do some skiing, but our boat was still in storage, and he said he'd be glad to take me around the lake a few times. He seems an all-right guy. What's the problem?"

"The problem, sweet brother, is that he's my boss."

"So?"

Cathy shook her head at him in warning. They were at the end of the dock but Cathy was sure Alex had not heard them. The low, powerful motor was already making a bubbling sound in the water. "Get in," Alex ordered crisply. "I'll turn around and you can toss the rope to him."

Her wooden sandals enabled her to climb into the boat with ease. The yellow nylon rope went snaking into the air to Cam.

He caught the rope, propped the tips of his skis up, and squatted in the water. "Ready."

Alex pushed the throttle forward and with a low growl, the boat surged ahead.

Cameron came up smoothly. Leaning back, he weaved from side to side, crossing the boat's wake. One hand lifted in a skier's salute and he grinned at Cathy. She settled into the bucket seat in the back, but when they were out on the lake and Cameron was skiing well, Alex glanced at her, frowned and said, "Come sit up in the front."

She hesitated and then moved into the leather seat next to him, turning to keep Cameron in view. Alex's profile was just within her peripheral vision. The wind blew his hair, lifting the silky black strands and whipping them against his ear and cheek. She leaned back against the front dash of the boat and tried to get comfortable, watch Cam—and shut Alex out of her vision. If it hadn't been for his disturbing presence less than a foot away, she would have reveled in the beauty of the June day. The sky seemed bluer than she had ever seen it, the trees on the surrounding hills a deep, healthy shade of green. A long, narrow sliver of water almost twenty miles long and only two miles wide, the lake was close to two cities and had been the scene of summer relaxation for years. The houses reflected that use. Old and new architectural designs were mixed together in a hodgepodge of A-frame and colonial, Victorian and ranch.

Alex twisted the wheel slightly, guiding the boat away from a catamaran that glided over the water on their starboard side, its deep purple and red rainbow-colored sail not quite taut in the light breeze. Cam gave the sailors, two young men, a high-flung wave. He turned back to Cathy and gave her a twisting wrist sign for one more turn-around.

"He's tireless, you know," she said. "He'll ski all day if you'll let him."

A slight smile lifted the male lips. "Are you in a hurry to go back to bed?"

"No. I just thought I'd warn you."

He studied her, his eyes greenlit with amusement. "Thanks for the warning, even though it isn't necessary. I intend to exact payment."

Something fluttered in her stomach. "Oh?"

He smiled a lazy smile. "Cam has offered to drive the boat and loan me his skis."

"You—water ski?"

"Does that surprise you?"

"Yes—I—"

One dark eyebrow arched. "Do you see me as a crippled old man?"

"No, of course not," she said quickly, in a light tone, refusing to think of the way she did see him. "I just wasn't aware you were familiar with the sport, that's all."

His face was expressionless. "I haven't skied lately."

She couldn't think of a reply. She stared out over the water, her eyes following Cameron, her thoughts on the man beside her. She could only imagine the pain he had suffered, psychological as well as physical. He had been at the height of his career—the young genius of Broadway. His direction assured a play's long-running success. Now at the age of thirty-five, when he should have been enjoying that success, he had to start over again. It wasn't surprising he had chided her for careless driving!

A turn of the wheel brought them around, and they cruised back down the side of the lake. When they neared Alex's A-frame house, Cathy said, "Is that someone on your dock?"

"Pamela, probably." He sounded indifferent. "She mentioned she might drop by this morning."

It was Pamela. The woman waved excitedly, and then Cathy

could see Devlin Smith standing just behind her. Alex sped by, unable to stop with Cameron behind. He made a wide turn, and then swung around so that Cameron could release the rope and drop into the water. When he turned the boat and pulled in close to the dock, Pamela hardly waited for the boat to stop moving before she put a long length of bare leg inside. She wore a green bikini sliced away at the hip and a lacy coverup that swung open as she moved, her full breasts pushing against the scanty patches of green silk. As she sat down on the padded leather seat she clutched the large brim of her straw hat and glanced around the luxurious interior of the boat. "Alex, this is fabulous." She turned to look at Cathy and her tinted amber sunglasses didn't hid the glint of antagonism in her eyes. "How nice you're here, Cathy. Devlin was delighted when he recognized you." To Alex, she said, "Let me sit up front with you, darling. I'm dying to see how everything works."

There was a loud splash. Cameron slid the skis up on the dock, heaved his body out of the water, and unzipped the life jacket. Alex nodded toward him. "You'll have to ask the new captain in command. I'm going for a turn around the lake."

Pamela frowned. "Alex, you aren't. Suppose you fall and break a leg. You know you're supposed to be careful—"

His tone was lightly laced with acid. "Save it, Pam." She subsided into silence at once and he climbed out of the boat and began to undress, stripping off his T-shirt unselfconsciously. He paused for a second and Cathy's heart accelerated. Then he stepped out of his jeans, and she knew why he had hesitated. A long white scar writhed up his right thigh and disappeared under the leg of his black form-fitting trunks. Scars marred the dark skin of his muscled calves. A confused jumble of feelings twisted through her—anger that he had suffered when he had not been at fault, pity, horror, and most of all a sense of shock in seeing the visible evidence of his brush with death.

He bent to pick up the yellow life jacket and as he straightened, he looked at her. His mouth thinned into a hard line. She knew at once that her eyes had betrayed her—and he had mistaken what he saw there. He thought she was repelled. She wasn't. It wasn't repugnance or disgust she felt. It was the shock of knowing that a quicksilver empathy had raced round her veins—almost as if she had, in that moment, suffered all the pain and anguish he had suffered.

Cameron climbed into the boat and bent over the console. "Okay, let's see. Throttle here. Gear shift here. I think I've got it." He lifted his head and smiled at Alex. "Any last minute instructions?" Alex turned to look at Cameron, and the cold hardness melted out of his eyes. "Just take it easy on the hills."

Cameron laughed. "Sure thing, Alex."

She sat in an intolerable state of tension as Cameron turned the boat and maneuvered it into position. Would just-healed sinew and bone stand that first pull as Alex bore down on legs and knees in order to come up out of the water?

No one said anything. Alex held the towline and Cameron sent the boat slowly ahead, pulling the rope taut.

"Ready," he called, and Cam pushed the throttle forward.

Cathy watched, her heart in her throat as Alex lifted himself into that uncomfortable half-crouch while the boat accelerated, pulling him through the water faster and faster. She held her breath. Suddenly he straightened. Pamela waved excitedly to him and began to relate to Devlin the details of Alex's accident. Cathy shut the woman's voice out of her mind and let herself breathe again. But her eyes never wavered from Alex. She was the observer, and it was her job to watch and tell Cameron if he fell, or gave the thumb-over-the-shoulder sign that he wanted to return to the dock. While she had never taken the responsibility of observing lightly, she had never felt it more heavily than she did now.

She watched Alex with the intensity of a hawk, but it was becoming clear that she worried unnecessarily. He had evidently been an expert waterskier before his accident, and his skills were returning. He swung from side to side behind the boat as Cameron had, but his muscular body leaned out even further at the end of each swing. His skis sliced the water and a shower of mist soared into the sky behind his head, diffusing the sunlight into a miniature rainbow. He suddenly swung far to the side, crouched, lifted his skis and jumped the wake. A cry of protest rose to her lips which she just barely stilled. Devlin and Pamela were turned watching Alex, and only Cameron saw her press her hand against her mouth.

"Did he fall?" Cameron's hands clenched on the wheel, ready to turn the boat.

"No." She told him what Alex had done. Cameron twisted his head around and watched as Alex executed another jump. "He is good, isn't he?"

"Just face front and watch where you're going, Cam."

His voice low, he teased, "You're afraid I'll dump your boss in the lake and you won't get your next paycheck."

Devlin Smith leaned forward and said in Cameron's ear, "Hey, any chance I could ski a round?"

"Ask him," Cam said, jerking his head in Alex's direction. "It's his boat." Cameron eyed the young man. "Have you ever done it before?"

"A few times." Devlin smiled at Cathy, his brown eyes admiring her. "Do you ski?"

"I know how, yes, but it's been ages. . . ."

"With a boat this size—we could ski at the same time."

Pamela looked from Devlin to Cathy, her mouth twisting in distaste. "You're all insane."

Alex lifted his hand and sketched the thumbs-back sign in the air, and Cameron circled and headed back to the dock. After Alex crawled out of the water, and shed skis and life jacket, he listened to Devlin's request to ski double with Cathy. His eyes flickered over her coolly. "Are you that good?"

She hadn't been convinced she really wanted to ski with Devlin. But Alex's soft challenge stiffened her resolve.

"I haven't skied in a few years—but it should come back to me."

"Before or after you break your neck?" His voice was softly mocking.

Irritated, she said sharply, "I can take care of myself."

His dark gaze inspected her face impersonally. "I don't have an extra tow line or a pair of skis."

"We've got them," Cameron told him, "but we'll have to go over and pick them up."

"We'll need another life jacket, too, Cam," she reminded him.

Cameron nodded. "You want to drive?" he asked Alex. Cathy could see her brother hated to relinquish the wheel of the powerful boat.

"You're doing a good job." He slid in between Cameron and Cathy on the front seat, his cool and moist body intolerably close. She moved, trying to create space between her tingling skin and his, and saw the leap of a muscle along his jaw.

"Darling, that was wonderful." From the back seat, Pamela leaned forward and brushed a droplet of water from his bare shoulder. He slanted around to Pamela, his wet thigh against Cathy. "Would you like to ski with me?"

"Alex, you know I can't risk getting a broken bone." Her trailing finger swirled a circle at his neck. Disturbed, Cathy looked away out over the water. An irrational anger heated her veins. He chided her about taking careless chances, yet he had risked injury to impress Pamela.

Cameron guided the boat around the promontory of land that divided Alex's house from their own. At the Taylor dock, Cameron handed the wheel over to Alex and jumped out.

He was back in minutes, carrying the extra skis and life jacket. Cathy climbed out of the boat beside Devlin and then realized she would have to stand on the dock and strip off her clothes just as Alex had.

She hesitated for a brief second, then faced away from the boat, quickly unknotted her blouse and pulled off her jeans. The maillot circled her body so that the back was not cut low, but she felt a burning between her shoulder blades, as if she could feel the heat of Alex's gaze on her bare shoulders just as she had that first night.

Devlin wore his bathing suit under his jeans, too, and stood and stripped unself-consciously. She doubted if he had ever been self-conscious about anything. He was young, possibly only a year or so older than Cameron, with dark, curly hair, the build of an athlete, and loads of practiced charm. She was sure he was well aware of the picture he made as he stood on the dock and grinned at her.

There was an odd little silence in the boat behind them. Then Pamela's cool voice said, "Alex, don't they make a handsome couple—both so dark-haired—and young?"

Cathy didn't wait to hear his reply. She zipped on the life jacket, rammed her feet into the skis, and slid them off the dock into the shallow water.

Devlin splashed in next to her, grinned and cocked his skis up just as she did. They each gripped a rope and nodded. The boat surged forward, pulling them up. Cameron increased speed and headed for the middle of the lake.

Because Cameron was driving, Alex acted as their observer, and Cathy felt his dark gaze on them every inch of the first round. She tried to forget him and enjoy the warm sun on her head and the cool water bathing her in a fine spray. She loved to ski; it gave her the feeling of being young again, of feeling that glorious sense of freedom and speed and sensual pleasure she loved as a teenager.

They skied conventionally side by side until Devlin suddenly leaned his upper body away and tilted his skis toward her, cutting the water and gliding so close she felt a light spray from his skis. He swung away, controlling his path with his powerful legs. She glanced at him and saw his broad smile. His grin was contagious, and she answered it, but she really wasn't interested in trying anything showy. The first round had been beautiful, but now she was beginning to remember that she hadn't skied in ages, and she could feel the pull of the boat in her arms and legs. She had to concentrate all her energy on staying on her feet. She wasn't afraid of a fall, but skiing double meant Devlin would have to be submerged when the boat slowed to pick her up again.

Devlin moved his grip higher on the rope, letting the triangle dangle under his wrist. "Let's criss-cross," he shouted. "Now!"

He skied toward her and she had no choice but to ski toward him and away from his destination. He ducked under her rope and went by her with a loud swish of moving water. She was not exactly steady, but she managed to change places with him and stay on her feet. At another signal from him, she crossed his path again, while he ducked under her towrope and went back to his own side.

Devlin repeated the action until she felt her knees begin to tremble and her arms ache from nervous strain.

"Stay where you are," he shouted, and she was only too glad to comply. Suddenly he was beside her, his voice raised to carry over the sound of the water and the boat motor. "Ever go piggyback?"

She shook her head. He skied close, and she knew she should protest, but before she could move or try to stop him, he slipped out of his right ski and stepped on the back of hers. His weight shifted, and then his other ski drifted away, and he was behind her, riding on her skis, his weight making them cut deeply into the water. He dropped his tow rope with one hand, put his arms tightly around her to grasp hers, and she was locked against him, the powerful muscles of his thighs straining against hers.

"Cozy, huh?" His voice laughed in her ear. "I knew sooner or later I'd get you in my arms."

Only their life jackets kept every inch of their bodies from touching. In the boat, Alex moved, and she saw that his face looked cold and closed.

The dark head turned toward Cameron. Cam shot a look over his shoulder and then turned toward Alex. He nodded and swung the boat around, carefully avoiding the path of another powerboat cutting across in front of them.

"Our esteemed director is unhappy," Devlin said in her ear. "I think he just told your brother to take us back to the dock. Give him the around-again sign."

Her arms felt as if they were being pulled out of their sockets.

"Really, I'd rather not—" She saw the dark blue troughs of the other boat's wake coming crosswise toward them, and there was nothing she could do to avoid the turbulent water. Her skis tipped down into a trough and then up again on the crest of the wave, and in a desperate attempt to compensate for Devlin's added weight, she leaned forward. She lost her balance and fell down on the incredibly hard surface of the water, her hand clinging to the tow rope with a death grip. Water surged into her face and all around her and an intolerable pain shot through her arm. Someone shouted, and she flung the rope away, only faintly aware that without it, Devlin was the heavy weight that was pushing her under the surface of the water.

CHAPTER SIX

She was under water. She thrashed in angry confusion and tried to get her head up to breathe. Her arms seemed useless. She surfaced, went under, closed her mouth to keep from inhaling water and told herself not to panic. She could swim. The problem wasn't swimming. The problem was breathing. Why did the life jacket seem to be pushing her down instead of lifting her up? She struggled, fighting to get free of the tangle of hard, unyielding material under her arms when suddenly, a cruel tug at the nape of her neck brought her head out of the water. She opened her mouth and gasped, sobbing in air. A hard, muscular arm clamped itself around her middle. "Cathy!"

The voice was harsh and strained but compelling. She opened her eyes. "Alex—" He floated in the water next to her, his shoulders beaded with moisture.

"Damn you! You could have been killed."

"Don't," she said, in an instinctive effort to protect herself from his harsh words. "Let go of me. I'm all right." He made a disbelieving sound, but he did release his painful hold on her hair. But now his free hand slid down to wrap itself around her waist and draw her almost into his arms. She raised her arm to fend off his watery embrace. "Ah—" Her cry of pain brought him even nearer, his legs tangling with hers.

"Don't move," he commanded her sharply. "Your arm might be broken."

She bobbed in his arms, confused and shaken. Every inch of his hard, wet flesh seemed to be touching her.

"Is she all right?" Devlin's face appeared above the water a few feet away.

"She's alive," came the rough answer. "No thanks to you."

"I didn't think she'd fall—"

"You didn't think at all," Alex shot back, harsh condemnation in his voice. The engine of the boat throbbed in the water. "Cut that motor," Alex ordered Cameron sharply. "There's a ladder under the rear seat." She heard the metallic sound as Cameron fastened the short metal ladder to the side of the boat. "Lay back in the water." Alex ordered.

She could take care of herself. "No—"

"Yes. Do it now!"

She was too exhausted to battle with that hard determination. She relaxed back and kept her eyes on the blueness of the sky as his arm shifted to clasp her around her waist, just under her breasts. He gave a kick with his powerful legs and they began to move through the water. It was then she knew she hadn't escaped injury. Pain knifed through her right arm from her elbow to her shoulder. Despite her discomfort, when they reached the ladder, she lifted her head and said "I can manage," and grasped the cool metal with her uninjured arm to hoist herself up.

From underneath a hard, warm hand fit around her bottom to boost her upward. Her face flamed, but no one seemed to notice her extraordinary color when Cameron helped her over the side and settled her into the front seat. "You okay, Cath?" His hazel eyes moved over her face, a worried frown between his brows.

"Just—shaken up a bit." She sank down and cradled her right arm, more aware than ever of the pain that was becoming a constant ache from shoulder to elbow.

Alex climbed into the boat, his body dripping water. He snatched up a heavy beach towel, but instead of drying himself off, he stepped to her side and wrapped it around her shoulders.

Don't, her mind cried. *Don't be considerate of me. Not now. Please just go away and leave me alone.*

But he didn't hear her silent plea, of course, and instead, he slid into the bucket seat beside her, taking infinite care not to bump her.

She tried to order her mind to be reasonable, knowing that if she stiffened, he would certainly suspect that his nearness disturbed her. She willed herself to relax, even though her nerves reacted to his presence like an alarm system that had been set off and was jangling in noisy confusion.

She was so intent on keeping herself under control that when a hand touched her from behind, she started. Devlin, a contrite look on his handsome face, moved his hand away reluctantly. "Cathy, I'm really sorry—"

"Devlin, for heaven's sake," Pamela said crisply. "She was wearing a life jacket. She couldn't possibly have drowned—"

"She could have if she had stayed unconscious for much longer. Five minutes is all it takes." Alex's chill tone quieted Pamela and created a silence in the boat that was heavy with unspoken thought. He turned to Cameron. "Take us back to the dock so we can pick up Cathy's clothes. Then I'll take her to the emergency room."

Pamela's soft tones floated up from behind them. "Darling, don't you think you're being—" a carefully timed pause, "intrusive?"

"She was skiing behind my boat when she was injured," Alex countered coldly.

A chill shivered over her skin. He was concerned because he felt responsible. If she needed an antidote to her feelings for Alex, that was a strong dose. She straightened and moved just enough so that she was no longer touching him. "I don't think I need medical attention—"

His eyes sliced over her. "That arm has to be X-rayed."

She leaned back in the seat. She was cold in the warmth of the sun and shocked and weary, but at least she was safe from her own unruly heart. "I suppose you're right," she agreed indifferently.

By the time they docked the second time, the pain in her arm had become unbearable and she no longer cared that Alex was at her side, helping her out of the boat. She was only dimly aware of Devlin apologizing once again, of Alex cutting him off with a curt direction to take Pamela home. To Cameron, he said, "Take the boat out and pick up the skis Smith dropped. I'll catch up with you later."

No one questioned any further his right to order them about, although Devlin's mouth compressed in a tight line as he climbed out and turned to help Pamela step onto the dock. They walked away together and, a few minutes later, as Alex propelled Cathy across the lawn and through the sliding glass door, the sound of their car leaving reached her ears.

"Can you walk upstairs?" His hand on her other arm was cool and impersonal.

"Why should I?"

He gestured at the glass wall behind them and a mocking smile curved his lips. "I thought you might not want to change here in full view of the population of Canandaigua Lake, but—if you don't mind—I'm sure I don't."

Unreasonable anger mixed with something else she didn't want to think about surged through her. "I see your point. If you'll just give me my clothes and point me in the right direction —"

The amused light in his eyes faded. He put the palm of his hand against her back, urging her forward. "Don't be ridiculous. You can't get out of that suit with an injured arm all by yourself."

His eyes played over the sleek fit of her suit, and new frissons of alarm tingled through her. Her reply was curt. "I'll manage."

He grasped her uninjured elbow and propelled her forward.

She climbed the steps beside him, her pulses pounding with a fierce resolve. He was the one acting ridiculous if he thought she would just let him undress her as if she were a doll or a clothing store dummy. She had to find a way to convince him she could manage.

At the top of the stairs the neat, liveable bedroom done in cream and brown silk that was his masculine domain did things to her nervous system. It was so—personal, seeing his bedroom. And to make things worse, her notes, the yellow legal paper filled with her handwriting, lay stacked neatly on the nightstand.

Before she could protest, he pushed her into the bathroom. Her eyes fastened on the oxblood leather shaving kit that stood open on the counter, the contents neatly arranged, razor, shaving cream, an expensive cologne with a famous designer's name. She was thinking how like him it was to be organized even in this—when she felt his hands grasp the top of her suit.

She summoned up her composure and made her voice chill. "I don't want your help."

"Why not?" he answered just as coolly. "I assure you your body holds no mysteries for me." He drawled the next words with a sardonic humor, "I have seen a woman's body before."

She didn't want to be reminded of that at this particular moment. She lifted her arm to ward him off, but pain stabbed her elbow, and she paled and gasped. Moving like lightning, he peeled her suit down over her breasts, hips and legs and was kneeling at her feet with the bit of wet silk draped around her ankles before she fully realized he had stripped her. He lifted first one foot and then the other out of the wet suit and tossed it on the edge of the bathtub. As he straightened, silence seemed to hum in her ears. His eyes swept down over her naked curves for a brief moment. Then his eyes returned to hers. She met his look steadily, her breathing shallow and forced. He made a low sound in his throat and turned away to rip a huge terry towel off the bar with unnecessary violence. It was then that shuddering reaction swept over her. She had wanted him to see her, wanted him to touch her. . . . He swathed her in the towel and began to rub her, his hands hard and impersonal on top of the terrycloth.

She couldn't emulate his detached attitude. His nearness and his warm breath on her bare neck made her nerves begin to vibrate again at a newer, higher frequency. And for no reason. He had seen every inch of her—and he had not been affected. It upset her to see his cool, almost clinical attitude. And then she was angry with herself, for the turn her thoughts had taken, for the aching desire she felt for him. She shuddered, and his hand went to the smooth bareness of her throat to tilt her head back and force her eyes to meet his. "You're in shock."

She wanted to laugh hysterically. The impulse to destroy his cool control made her ask huskily, "Is that what it is?"

His eyes traveled her face, searching each feature, silently questioning the low sensuality throbbing in those words. She returned his look honestly, her need there in the violet eyes for him to see. "Alex," she whispered, unable to keep his name from her lips.

He groaned softly, and hard hands flattened themselves against her back and forced her against his taut body. "You do pick your time, don't you?" His mouth came down with a punishing kiss that swept her mind clear of everything but his warm, nearly naked body against her own.

He demanded her response and she couldn't deny him. She couldn't deny him access to the warmth of her mouth. She gave herself freely, meeting his passion with a fierce need of her own.

A shudder and tensing of his muscles warned her he was going to end the kiss. His lips against her cheek, her murmured, "How warm and real you are. Cathy, I—"

"No." She shook her head. Words were an intrusion. She wanted his mouth on hers again, wanted that feeling of complete wholeness, wanted to know that her lips were as enticing to him as his were to her. "Don't talk." She pressed against him. "Please . . . kiss me again."

He gazed down at her, not moving, his body tense, his facial bones hard against the tanned skin. He was fighting the sweet enticement of her swollen mouth, the heady invitation in her husky voice. She pressed closer, her breasts brushing the dark springy hair that grew on his chest, her hand tracing the warm contours of his mouth.

His resistance collapsed. Hungrily, as if those few seconds away from her had intensified his desire for her, he took her lips with a warm, persuasive tenderness, an evocative possession that banished everything from her mind but the thought that she wanted him more than she had ever wanted any man in her entire life. In his arms, his hands a delight on her bare back, his tongue making erotic forays into the depths of hers, she was complete as she had never been before.

She let her own hands discover the smooth silk of his back, and felt the sheathed muscles underneath move as he adjusted his hold to ensure her comfort.

This time, when he lifted his head, she moved to maintain her contact with him. Her mouth sought the firm line of his jaw, traced down his throat and wandered lower to nestle in the soft hollow.

He groaned. "Cathy, I'm warning you—"

The vibrating sound of his voice lay just under her lips, tantalizing her like the purr of a kitten.

"Alex—" She raised her eyes to him, and as he read the message of sweet submission, flames leaped into his own.

He scooped her up, towel and all, and swung out of the bathroom with her. Carrying her over to the bed, her laid her gently on the spread, and leaned over her to draw the towel away. His eyes caressed her feminine beauty. "I've wanted you here—" his eyes, gleaming with laughter, moved around the bed and then came back to shine their brilliance on her, "—since the first moment I saw you."

She lifted her hand to touch his mouth once again. "Alex." Her voice was a soft invitation.

He groaned and reached for her, cupping her breast with tenderly explorative fingers. Light and heat seemed to burst inside her. Aching need centered deep within her, clamoring for appeasement. His hip, clad only in the thin swim suit, nudged hers as he sat down and leaned over her, his hands still moving with erotic ease over her breasts.

His hand left her rosy bud, and she made a soft, protesting sound at the loss, only to gasp with delight when he bent over her and trailed his lips over the taut line of her throat. He ended his journey at the curve of her breast, and there, he slowed his pace, nuzzling the slopes and silken textures of her, nibbling at the satiny skin. He held her in suspense, exploring the valleys, but not the peaks, witholding that final-earthshaking claiming of her nipple, purposely building the intolerable anticipation.

She buried her fingers in the dark, silky hair at his neck, feeling as if each strand was a silken gift for her alone. His hands moved slowly over her hips, his warm mouth searing a trail of fire across her abdomen and down the long curve of her thigh, teaching her pleasures she hadn't thought possible, giving her ecstasy she had only glimpsed in dreams.

"Alex, please. Have a little mercy—"

"No," he murmured, his voice low and husky and disturbed. "No mercy."

His voice was a spoken caress that made her yearn to touch him and claim him as he was claiming her. She dropped her hand from his neck to massage his heavily muscled shoulders against her sensitive palms, loving the smell of him, that fresh, clean scent of his cologne mingled with the musky male scent of him.

His tongue resumed teasing her breast. Then, suddenly, without warning, his mouth covered the swollen peak possessively. She gasped with delight and clutched his dark head as aching need centered deep within her and radiated outward in ever-wider circles. Her hands wandered lower down his back. She traced the straight line of his spine, found the firm, taut curves of his buttocks, and the beginning of scarred flesh along his thigh.

He moved closer and lifted his mouth to kiss her again. This time his tongue claimed her boldly, thrusting against hers, taking pleasure from her as if he was a buccaneer pirate. She moved her hips in silent provocation, and with a deep-throated groan that seemed to echo inside her own mouth, he moved over her.

Pain shot through her arm. She cried out in surprise more than distress. She had been so absorbed in pleasure she had forgotten her injury. Alex lifted his hands from her at once. "My God! I must be out of my mind!" He pulled away.

She stared at him in an agony of need and desire, but he braced his hands on the side of the bed and got to his feet quickly, as if driven. When he had disappeared into the bathroom, she huddled under the towel, and felt very little better when he returned with her clothes in his hand.

He sat down on the bed and said matter-of-factly. "Sit up and give me your arm."

Dear God, how could he turn his emotions off and on like that? His eyes were hooded, but his hands on her arm were cool. Even his coolness couldn't take the heat away. Her body still throbbed with an unfulfilled ache. But his had been a desire of the moment only.

She did as he asked, and even though he was gentle, she winced as he slid her blouse up over her shoulder. When the garment was on, his hands went to the front tie. As he tied the silk, his fingers brushed the deep sensitive valley between the curve of her breasts, but there was not a flicker of reaction in his face. Desperately, she fought to be as cool.

He put her feet into her jeans with the same silent control, as if he had never come close to possessing her. When she was dressed, he lifted her to her feet with consummate care. "Can you walk downstairs by yourself?"

She would. She had to, even though her stomach was churning and her mind not functioning. "Of course." She forced unwilling legs to stand and carry her forward. It took every ounce of her concentration. Her mind was too distressed to think of anything else but those moments in Alex's arms.

"I'll be down as soon as I've dressed," he said matter-of-factly, and she turned to walk down the stairs.

The air was heavy with summer heat when they got into the car minutes later. She felt like a hollow puppet controlled by unseen strings. Why had she made her desire for him so obvious—why? She had given herself away completely. She raked a hand through the still-damp hair that was tumbled from his lovemaking and settled in the cream upholstery, wishing she had never seen this car—or the man who owned it.

The numbness and shock wore off—and in its place came a sick self-loathing. Alex may have been caught up in his desire for the moment, but that was all. His quick release of her and his calm deliberate movements as he dressed her told her plainly how little his emotions were involved.

She felt depressed and degraded, and her state of mind hadn't changed when they reached the hospital. The emergency room was small and clean and medicinal smelling, the doctor cheerful and philosophic. After he had looked at the X rays, he told her, "You're a lucky young lady, Ms. Taylor. Nothing's broken. You've dislocated the joint at your elbow, but it's already back in place. Keep your arm supported for the rest of the day and don't do anything strenuous. You'll ache tonight but you'll be better tomorrow. Take aspirin and rest for the remainder of the day."

Alex was as silent on the trip back to her father's house as he had been earlier, but when he pulled into the circular driveway and stopped the car, he said tersely, "Sit still. I'll come around and let you out."

When he did so, she found his hand on her elbow made her legs more unsteady, not less. She winced as she got out of the car.

His mouth tightened. "This wouldn't have happened if you weren't so intent on exhibiting your—skills for young Smith to admire."

Her voice cold, she denied it. "I wasn't—showing off for him."

"Weren't you?" He stood staring down at her. The late afternoon shadows of the trees moved in an intricate pattern over his dark face. "He's been looking for an excuse to make a play for you for days."

"You're imagining things." In an effort to lighten the situation and say the expected thing, she said, "Thank you for taking me to the hospital." She hesitated and then added, "Actually, I suppose it was to your benefit. Now I have no reason to miss rehearsal."

"You're not going anywhere tonight but to bed."

"There isn't any reason I can't come to the theatre—"

"There's a very good reason," Alex said coolly. "I don't want you there."

"I see," she said stiffly, knowing that if their positions were reversed, she would have insisted that he be with her tonight . . . and later. . . .

His face was engimatic. "You really are . . . impossible at times, do you know that? I'll see you tomorrow."

She turned to go into the house, blocking the sound of that cool, slightly mocking voice out of her mind as she climbed the steps.

The pungent odor of fresh coffee filled the air. In front of her, the cast was walking through the play. Alex sat next to her and watched them with an attention that was frightening in its single-mindedness.

She gripped the legal pad and absently rubbed her arm. It had been three days since the accident and her arm was better. Unfortunately, the same could not be said for her mental condition.

She had been ready for anything from Alex that first night at work after the accident on the lake—anything, that is, except his polite indifference. After two evenings of that, she had had to clench her hands together on the way home in the car to keep from flying at his face and raking it with her nails, making him admit her existence as more than a note-taking automaton. She wanted him to remember that they had once nearly been as close as a man and a woman could be. Then common sense took hold. How could she work with him if she were both emotionally and physically involved with him? Being emotionally drawn to him was bad enough. It would be a thousand times worse if he realized exactly how she felt—and pressed his advantage. If only she could forget the ecstasy he had given her . . .

She clenched her hands in her lap and tried to concentrate on the play. Alex was silent in the seat beside her, which was a good thing. She doubted if she could have put one coherent thought down on paper.

Focusing her eyes steadily on the stage and blocking Alex out of her peripheral vision, she leaned back in the plush seat. She had to admit that working with Alex had given her insights into the theatre she never would have gained any other way. Somehow, after sitting next to him, listening to his comments, her eye had become keener, more discerning. She had learned to look at the play as a whole. Right now, Devlin was teetering back and forth on his heels while Barbara read her lines. How long would Alex tolerate that?

Barbara finished her speech and moved hesitantly upstage, almost as if she sensed she did not have Alex's attention. In a voice that sliced the silence Alex said, "Igor, you are concerned about Toni, intrigued by her, worried about her. Do you think you could possibly stand still while she delivers a line?"

The young man mumbled, "Sorry." He swept a nervous smile around the stage.

"Let's break," Alex said, and without a pause, turned to her. "I've talked with Simon," he said, his voice low, his quick mind switching to the topic of his stage manager. "He's going out of town this weekend to see his wife. He had planned on putting the final touches on the scenery. Can you cover for him?"

"Yes," she said coolly.

"There are a couple of doors that need to be touched up. If you have Saturday afternoon free and can come to the theatre, I'll stop by and pick you up. We'll probably be working late—I'll take you out to dinner after we're through."

"That won't be necessary," she said calmly. "I'm sure you have other things to do. . . ."

The flare of anger in his eyes warned her not to continue. He turned away and pushed himself up out of the seat and was halfway down the aisle toward the stage before she realized she was alone.

After the break rehearsal began again, and Alex sat in the theatre watching the stage action. Cathy could see he was becoming more dissatisfied by the minute. At last he straightened out of his seat and walked down the aisle. "Smith, haven't you ever danced with a woman you loved?"

Devlin kept a smile glued to his lips. "You mean recently?"

"Anytime, now—ever," Alex responded impatiently. "You're

holding Pamela as if you're afraid she'll break. Get a good grip on her. She won't bend out of shape. Here, let me show you."

He ignored the steps and swung lithely up on the stage. Devlin released Pamela to him and stood off to the side, his face a study in control.

His lean hand grasping her by the wrist, Alex drew Pamela forcefully into his arms. In the darkened auditorium, Cathy clenched her teeth and felt the clip of the pen she held cut into the fleshy part of her hand before she realized she had tightened her hold on it. Slowly, deliberately, Alex pressed Pamela closer until they were melded together. The actress had worn a halter top and brief white shorts and as Alex began to dance with her, he placed his hand deliberately on the bare small of her back and brought their entwined hands up to nestle them against his chest.

Cathy fought to contain the bitter churning in her stomach. She could feel her expression hardening and tried to force her eyes away from the stage—but she couldn't. She could only watch in fascination as Alex moved with Pamela in a slow, sensuous rhythm, their legs intimately entwined. Then she heard him say to Devlin, "You're younger than Stephanie—" Pamela raised her face and gave Alex a sardonic, knowing look, "but that doesn't make any difference to you. You've just made the marvelous discovery that she's a beautiful and desirable woman, and you can't take your eyes off her. For you, everyone else in the room has ceased to exist." His eyes never left Pamela's face and her own softened into smiling approval.

There was a heavy silence in the theatre. Cathy knew that the rest of the cast were seeing what she had known from the first—that Alex found it easy to look like a man in love—when he held Pamela Field in his arms. And perhaps that was his purpose. Was he showing Devlin that Pamela belonged to him, warning him away?

The possibility seemed even more likely after the rehearsal ended when Cathy saw Alex lingering to speak to Pamela. Unable to watch the dark head bent so close to the fair one, she rose from her seat, walked up the aisle, and out of the theatre. At the bottom of the steps a hand caught her arm. She turned, a sharp word on her lips, expecting to see Alex. But it was James who stood there in the dark night and looked down at her. She couldn't read the expression on his face, but his words were soft and touchingly hesitant.

"Since we don't have rehearsal tomorrow night—will you have dinner with me?"

She stared at him, seeing only the outline of his broad shoulders in the light of the vapor lamp. He had taken her completely by surprise.

"I—I'm sorry, James. I—have to work on the scenery and I don't know how long it will take. . . ."

"We'll make it late, say around nine."

She hesitated. She opened her mouth to say no—when the mental picture of Alex and Pamela dancing on the stage together rose in her mind. She couldn't bear spending an evening with Alex, knowing that he had nearly made love to her—while he still loved Pamela. She took a breath. "Thank you, James. I'd—I'd like that."

He reached for her hand. "I'll look forward to it, Cathy," he said with a tender gravity in his voice that touched her.

A sound behind her warned her the instant before Alex and Pamela descended the steps and came to stand beside them. She forced a smile to her lips and turned to them.

Pamela had her arm linked in Alex's and she turned up to him, a smile lifting her curved lips. "Why don't you come over tomorrow afternoon, darling, and we'll run over that part you're so unhappy with?" Pamela's voice was warm and caressing.

Alex shook his head. "I'll be doing scenery with Cathy and then I'm taking her out to dinner."

She shouldn't have been surprised that he really had meant to take her out—but she was.

"But Cathy's just agreed to have dinner with me." James's protest was soft but firm.

Saved from having to make any explanation by James's interjection, she saw the slight twist that lifted Alex's lips. "I believe she's committed to me for the evening, Carson."

Ever the diplomat, James turned to the frowning Pamela. "Why don't we make it a foursome then—if you'd care to join us, Ms. Field."

If Pamela disliked being an afterthought, she didn't show it. She smiled and said, "What a marvelous idea."

It wasn't a marvelous idea. Alex had called her that morning and said he wouldn't be able to make it to the theatre that afternoon, so she painted doors alone, her stomach churning in apprehension.

That night, her nerves hadn't calmed. She combed her hair, thinking she was glad she had the buffer of James between Alex and herself when the doorbell chimed. She hurried down the stairs to open it, a smile on her face to greet James. But the man who stood on her doorstep with a slightly mocking smile meeting her own was not James.

Alex was as elegant as he had been that night at Audrey's dinner party. Somehow, the sophisticated gray suit suited him exactly. He wore the vest buttoned, but the jacket swung loosely around his slim hips as he took a step toward her. Cathy thought fleetingly that no one had the right to look quite so attractive.

"Hello, Cathy."

There was an echoing self-mockery in those two words she didn't understand. "Hello, Alex." She came out of the house and closed the door. When she turned, she thought his sardonic look had deepened. The lines around his mouth were more noticeable, the attractive curve of his lips slightly drawn to one side. He scrutinized her, as if committing to memory every detail of her soft lime-green silk blouse and cream skirt. She avoided his eyes and led the way down the porch steps. When she stood by the car, the ruffles that framed the deep V neckline caught in the summer breeze and covered the creamy silk skin of her throat.

He opened the door for her. She settled in the front seat thinking that very soon James and Pamela would be joining them and she could relax, when he turned to her and his hand went to her throat. Before she could move or protest, his fingers repositioned the silk ruffle back over her breast where it belonged.

"There," he murmured with a self-satisfied sound, his hand lingering to trace the V neckline to its deepest point, "that throat is much too beautiful to hide."

The brush of his fingers in the valley of her breasts tantalized her, making her remember his caresses on her naked skin with a clarity that brought anguish—and anger. "Don't feel you're required to make an obligatory pass at your assistant, Alex."

Answering anger glittered in the green depths. "If that's what you think, I might as well do a good job of it . . ."

He grasped her shoulders, pulled her roughly to him, and brought his mouth down to clamp it on hers. Even in his anger, though, she could feel the restraint, the unwillingness to genuinely hurt her. And it was that, in the end, that was her undoing. He would never hurt her; she knew that instinctively. He had a cool containment during rehearsals that she had been admiring for weeks. That same awareness, that innate courtesy was softening his lips now, making his touch pure pleasure on her shoulders and back—a pleasure that was coaxing a response from her lips. She lifted her arms to his neck, her will to resist destroyed.

He lifted his mouth and gazed at her in the dim light, a caressing finger touching the end of her nose. "With all your talent, you can't hide it, can you? Your body tells me the truth. You want me as badly as I want you."

She stared up at him. "Wanting—and being used—are two different things."

Even in the darkness she saw his brows draw together. "What are you talking about?"

"I won't be used to ease your frustration for Pamela," she said, her voice low.

There was a long, silent moment. "How did you come up with that hare-brained assumption?"

"It's perfectly clear to anyone with eyes in their head to watch you—"

"And have you been?" There was the purr of a satisfied tiger in his voice.

She didn't answer. She wedged her hands between them and tried to push him away. He was hard and solid, an immoveable object. "How," he said softly, "have you managed to survive in this business with that naive outlook? And by what illogical process did you come to the conclusion that I'm nursing a grand passion for Pamela?"

"You loved her—before," she murmured.

"No," he said flatly. "I won't deny that there was a time when we—well, never mind. But there has never been an emotional commitment between us of any kind. We both knew the rules of the game."

"Is that what it is to you—a game?"

The dark lashes dropped down over his eyes. "There's an—element of that in any relationship between a man and a woman, isn't there? The zinging excitement of meeting someone new, the tantalizing thought of exploring another's mind—and body . . ."

Resolutely, she turned away from him and forced her unwilling muscles to stiffen. Her withdrawal brought a low sound of disgust from Alex. He released her and started the car and she sat next to the window, silent and shaken, hardly conscious of the direction he took out of the driveway as the thoughts churned inside her. He was a terrifying breed of man, a predator who saw women as intriguing prey. She thought that somehow it all related to his talent as a director. His ability to stand outside himself and observe others was frightening.

He took her to a small country inn high on a hill. It was made of pine logs and exuded a woodsy, homey atmosphere, but she felt a flicker of unease when they were escorted to an intimate, candlelit table for two next to the window. She sat down and was captivated immediately by the view. From the inn's height, she could look down on almost all of the lower half of the lake. The water shimmered in dancing, silvery waves in the moonlight. Lights from houses outlined the shore with answering brilliance.

She gazed, fascinated. But after a moment, she turned her head to glance around the small dining room, and the niggling alarm increased. What was keeping James and Pamela? She turned her head back to Alex and saw that sardonic gleam in his eyes grow brighter.

"Oh, yes, I forgot to tell you about the others," he said casually, picking up the silver menu. "Carson got a call from his wife and decided to take a flight to New York. Pamela discovered at the last minute she had—other plans."

The blood seemed to rush to her head. She would never have consented to come had she known they were going to dine *á deux.*

He glanced at her over the menu. "Do I take it that you are leaving it to me to order for both of us?"

"No." With determination, she picked up the menu. She stared at it, not reading a word.

"The duck is supposed to be excellent—"

Her stomach did a flip-flop. "No, thank you."

"The fish, perhaps?"

"I'll have a small steak and a salad. No potato."

"Cocktail?"

"I'd like a gin and tonic—double lime."

When the waiter appeared, Alex ordered her drink and then said, "Scotch on the rocks for me please."

The waiter went away, and the quiet lengthened. She kept her head turned, looking out the window.

"If I had known the view was going to give me that much competition, I'd have asked for another table."

She gave him a fleeting glance and averted her eyes. She had been caught, and she knew it.

The waiter came with the drinks and set them on round coasters before he went discreetly away.

He gave her a slicing glance. "Are you disappointed because Carson isn't here?"

She lifted the glass to her lips and felt the cool bite of lime on her throat. She replaced the glass carefully on the table. "No."

She gave him a direct look. Two could play at this game. "Are you disappointed because Pamela isn't here?"

He leaned back in his chair a cool, mocking smile on his lips. "No."

She couldn't disguise the slight expression of disbelief that flickered across her face, and Alex saw it.

"Does that surprise you?"

She didn't answer.

"I've already told you I'm not involved with Pam."

"It would hardly be wise to admit that you were."

If her words angered him, he didn't show it. Soft music began to filter through the sound system. The couple behind them rose and went to the tiny square of a dance floor.

"If I ask you to dance will you refuse?"

In her mind, she saw Pamela in Alex's arms. "Yes."

"Then I won't ask." He got to his feet. "I'll insist." He grasped her hand and brought her to her feet. There was little she could do but follow him, if she didn't want to cause a scene.

At the edge of the floor he turned and took her in his arms. As an actress she had learned to control her body and her emotions, but none of the things she had learned kept her from feeling that leap of exhilaration in every nerve of her body. She hadn't danced with anyone for a long while and she had forgotten how it felt to be held by a man who knew exactly how to hold a woman in his arms. She was conscious of everything about him, the rough-smooth cloth of his jacket, the scent of his cologne, the warmth of his hands on hers, the lean strength of his body. She was heady with lightness, a sense of belonging.

The music ended. Alex held her for a moment longer. Then he released her and smiled down into her face. "Perhaps we'd better go back to our table."

Had she been standing there looking at him with a bemused expression for very long? His slight smile told her that she had. Flushing, she turned and stepped away from him.

The food came and it was hot and delicious, but her appetite was gone. She went through the motions of eating but her mind vibrated with awareness of him, the way his hands moved as he ate his meal, the way his mouth fit on the lip of the wine glass.

She was sipping her wine when Alex said, "Is something wrong?"

"No—I'm just not hungry."

"Not very talkative, either."

With a smile lifting her lips, she murmured, "Isn't that why you hired me as your assistant?"

He gave her a shrewd look and didn't respond. "How do you think it's going?"

She hesitated and then said, "Very well."

"The weak spot is Smith."

That had been her own private observation exactly. He continued, "I have a feeling he'll come through in front of an audience."

"What makes you think that?"

He lifted one eyebrow. "Long experience with his type."

"Do you believe in types?"

He gazed at her thoughtfully. "If you observe the human race carefully—you begin to see certain behavior patterns repeat themselves."

She sat silent, her fingers playing over the cool stem of her wine glass. He had catalogued Devlin—and her as well.

"There is, of course, always an exception to the rule. There are those people who appear to be one thing, but really aren't." He gazed at her. "Pamela, for instance."

Disturbed, she echoed, "Pamela?"

"She appears to be a typical selfish leading-lady type. But underneath the facade, she's a frightened woman. She's growing older. Roles are not coming her way as they once did."

Before she could fully absorb that, he added softly, "And then there's you."

She was stilled by alarm. "What about me?" When he hesitated, she said coolly, "Do you still believe I'm nursing a father complex?"

He smiled a faintly mocking smile. "I'd be a fool to answer that—and risk losing a valuable employee."

Chill shivered over her skin. "Yes, of course."

His face darkened with irritation. "Really, Cathy," he sighed. "Somehow we've got to keep our personal relationship separate from our working one."

"We don't have a personal relationship," she murmured.

"How sure you sound." A muscle moved on the side of his jaw. "But I'll prove you wrong one day." He signaled the waiter. "Two coffees, please."

She wanted only to escape but when the coffee arrived, she placed her hands around the cup and tried to absorb its warmth. Alex poured cream into his and stirred it absently. "How's Cameron?"

"Fine." She wasn't up to polite conversation.

"And your father?"

"I'm sure he's healthy, if that's what you mean."

"You haven't spoken to him since the night of the dinner party?"

She stiffened. "Is that a question? If it is, I hardly think it's any of your business."

"Let's just say I'm still—curious."

"You know what they say about curiosity," she shot back.

"Being curious about people has its justifications at times." He leaned back in his chair, his eyes never leaving her face. "Barbara Stanton is expecting a child."

She inhaled sharply in surprise.

Alex nodded grimly. "Exactly. When I expressed concern about her emotional state the other evening—she told me."

"But she can still perform—"

"Under normal circumstances, she could. But she's been under a strain. Her doctor has warned her that if she continues to work all day and rehearse at night, she runs the risk of losing the baby. To make matters worse, she hasn't told her husband yet. She thinks if she does—he'll insist that she quit the play immediately.

"But we have no understudy—"

"She's determined to finish *Cactus Flower.* But she won't be able to do *The Wild Duck.*"

"Who will you get to play Hedvig?"

He gazed at her, his heavy dark lashes half hooding his eyes. "I want you to take over the role."

CHAPTER SEVEN

She stared at him. "Are you serious?"

"I'd hardly be anything else at this late date. The Ibsen goes into rehearsal next Monday night."

She clenched her hands in her lap and ordered her shocked brain to think. "Could—could I have some time to think it over?"

He frowned. "Think it over? Why would you need to do that?"

"I'm not sure—I can do it."

"Don't be ridiculous. Of course you can."

"You're very sure—"

He replied smoothly, "I've already auditioned you."

"What about the committee?"

"My contract stipulates that I have the authority to choose any replacements that become necessary. Well?"

"I—don't know."

His lips tightened. He pulled out a bill and laid it on top of the check. "Shall we go?"

His impatient mood chilled her blood and when they walked out to the car, she shivered slightly even though the summer breeze was warm and caressing. Inside the car, he shrugged out of his jacket. "Here, put this around you."

His fingers brushed her shoulders as he settled the jacket around her. Under his vest, his silken shirt gleamed like pale cream in the diffused light from the moon. He started the car, and she tried to concentrate on the lights from the dash, one large round one and three smaller circles of light. Inevitably, though, her eyes were drawn to his face illuminated in those tiny spots of light. How had he escaped facial injury in that accident? The hard line of his jaw was clean and firm, the lean cheek unscarred.

"Getting warmer?"

"Yes."

The scent of his jacket surrounded her. The firm strength of his hands on the wheel made her cheeks burn with longing.

Her mind churned with conflicting emotions. Hedvig was a classic and difficult role. She had understudied in Ibsen plays, but never performed them. The rest of the cast already knew their lines. She would have to learn the role quickly, perhaps in the next two days. And if she failed . . . she would severely jeopardize Alex's career. . . .

He slowed the car as they approached his house. "What are you doing?"

"Stopping off to get a script for you."

"I haven't said I'd do it."

He pulled into the driveway and stopped the car. With a flick of his wrist, he turned off the ignition. The night was suddenly alive with summer sounds, crickets chirping, the whisper of the lake against the shore, the rustle of the cottonwood leaves brushing against each other.

"You'll do it," he murmured. He got out of the car and came around to open her door. "Come on. I'll help you get started."

Clutching at his jacket with cool, nerveless fingers, she swung her feet out of the car. The breeze toyed with her silky skirt, making it swirl up around her thighs. She hastily smoothed it down but not before his eyes took in the long length of silken leg. She fought for composure and somehow achieved a semblance of calm as he brushed past her to close the car door.

Inside the house, he flipped a switch and light gleamed off the cream velvet couch. "Sit down. I'll only be a moment." When he ran up the stairs with his slightly off-beat, yet lithe step, she slipped his jacket from her shoulders and laid it over the low back of the sofa. Hesitantly, she glanced round the room. At night, it was even more attractive, intimately comfortable, cool, and inviting.

She was still standing there when he came down holding the two black bound scripts. He gave her a quick look, and then grasped her elbow and guided her to the sofa where he pushed her gently down on the cushions.

After he handed her one of the scripts, his fingers went to his vest. He unbuttoned and shrugged out of it, tossing it casually on the couch. The low table was pushed back and he lowered himself to the floor at her feet to lean against the front of the couch, his broad shoulder in the cream silk shirt disturbingly close to her thigh.

"Are you familiar with the play?"

A wooden movement of her head passed as a nod. "Then we'll start with the second act. I'll read the other roles." His eyes raked over her, commanding her to open the book and begin.

She sat utterly still. Weeks ago, she had longed for this moment. But weeks ago, Alex Reardon had been only a name, not the flesh and blood man that sat at her feet, lean and male and disturbingly attractive.

He gazed at her in silent command. She glanced away from his eyes nervously, and for something to do, paged through until she found the second act. The scene opened with Gina, the mother, calling Hedvig.

Alex began to read the role. He wasn't imitating the quality of a woman's voice, but his tone carried that unique blend of irritation and indulgence with which a mother might call her child. She had known he was a consummate actor, but somehow, hearing him raised the hair on the back of her neck. He was good, terribly, bone-chillingly good.

She sat silent and frozen.

"Cathy—"

She tossed the script on the table, jumped to her feet and went to the sliding glass door where she stood hugging her arms around her middle and peering out into the darkness, as if the sight of the lake was a talisman to keep her safe. But it wasn't.

All she could see was her own reflection. "I can't do it. You'll have to find someone else."

His voice was as clear and cold as spring water and its sound and direction told her he was still sitting on the floor where she had left him. "What do you mean—you can't do it?"

"I can't, that's all. I'm sorry . . ."

"Can't—or won't?" Suddenly he was behind her, his reflection merging with hers in the glass the instant before she felt his hard hands on her arms. Roughly he turned her around to face him. "What are you afraid of, Cathy?"

"Nothing—everything. Please, don't ask me to do this."

"Why?"

He was angry, and she felt it through his fingertips—as if they were transmitting his fury from the soft flesh of her upper arms directly to her brain. She trembled, but did not answer.

Coldly, he said, "This is an opportunity most young actresses would give their eye teeth for. Are you refusing it because of me?"

Yes, she wanted to cry. *Yes. Because I can't run the risk of failing you.* But she said nothing.

"Somehow, I hadn't pictured you as vindictive." The words were soft and menacing.

Roused from her silent trance, she echoed, "Vindictive?"

"You're taking your revenge, aren't you?"

"I don't know what you're talking about. . . ."

He pulled her closer. "You haven't forgiven me for what I said about Warren—have you?"

The color drained away from her face, leaving her paler than ever in the soft light. "You can't possibly believe I'm capable of that—"

"I think you're capable of almost anything."

Searing anger shot through her. "Perhaps I am—except playing this role well enough to suit you."

His fingers tightened on her arms, and then he released her suddenly as if his control would snap if he didn't stop touching her. "You're more than capable." He gazed at her with narrowed eyes. "Don't let the bitter feelings you hold against me destroy a chance at furthering your career."

"Damn you, Alex!" Yes, her feelings for him were getting in the way. Feelings he had totally misread. She was furious and threw digression to the wind. "Hasn't it occurred to you that if I fall flat on my face—the critics wouldn't blame me? They'd say it was because you'd lost your touch!"

Her words seemed to penetrate him slowly. "I must admit that didn't—occur to me." His eyes burned over her face as he took a step toward her. "It's me you're afraid for, not yourself." His face held comprehension and cool assessment, and she knew at once that she had betrayed herself.

"So if anything goes wrong," he went on relentlessly, "at least you won't be responsible—is that it?" He gave her a long, enigmatic look. "Have you so little faith in my ability?"

"It isn't your ability . . ."

"Or your own . . . there's something else, isn't there?" he went on with his cold line of reasoning. "You're afraid because of our personal relationship." He reached out and grasped her wrist, drawing her resisting body close to his.

"We don't have a personal relationship," she denied desperately.

"That's the second time you've denied that tonight," he countered coolly. "But no amount of denials, however expert your delivery, can change what we both know, what we both feel. Nothing can change the truth, Cathy." His outward calm was belied by the intensity of his tone. She pressed her hands to his chest only to feel herself drawn closer, to feel her body become more acutely aware of his. He looked at her long and hard until she felt her entire self being heated by his searching gaze. "Do you imagine yourself . . . in love with me?"

Stunned that he could read her thoughts so easily, fighting to hide the response she couldn't let him see, "Let go of me, Alex."

"But of course you won't answer that, will you? You lock your emotions away—and let them surface only when you're on stage." She struggled, trying to escape him. He tightened his grip and went on softly, "When I auditioned you, I couldn't believe all that fire was inside you. You hide it well in your everyday life." Another curious look. "Why, I wonder? Why are you so afraid to be yourself? Is it because you feel things so deeply you're terrified to let them show?" His eyes glinted with dangerous speculation. "Ah, now, there's a thought. Cathy Taylor with all her emotions laid bare." He drew her closer, his green eyes lit with pale lights of determination. "Your eyes give you away, did you know that? And you're not used to being understood, are you? You loathe it with all your being that you've given me a window into your soul. Right now, you resent the very fact that I exist. What would you like to do to me right now, Cathy? Kill me? Or make love to me?"

She felt coldly exposed, more naked than as if he had ripped the clothes from her body. "I think," she got out through gritted teeth, "that I could very cheerfully wring your neck."

They stared at each other in the long silence. "Then do it," he invited her softly. "Put your hands around my throat—and do it!"

He released her but didn't step away. "I'll even make it easier for you." He unbuttoned his shirt slowly, watching her. The tanned flesh came into view, then the darker hair near his navel. Her throat constricted. The memory of the time he had nearly made love to her in his bed washed over her.

Panicked, she moved to brush past him, but he caught her hands and swung her around. In the next instant, he had pressed her hands to the hard cords of his neck, his own hands trapping her fingers.

A heady heat rose inside her. His flesh was warm and smooth under her hands, his throat taut. Her chest burned, she couldn't breathe. She pulled her hands away and whirled to the patio door. She was fumbling with the clasp when he caught her.

"Cathy!"

He turned her into his arms and pulled her against him. She pushed at his chest ineffectively, crying and gasping in her fury, her fists pressing against his shoulders.

When her temper was spent and her breasts heaving with her gasping breaths, he gathered her closer. "Cathy—" He bent his head.

But her mouth was not his destination. He caught her cold hands and brought them up to his lips in a curiously old-world gesture of respect and affection. "You couldn't harm me," he murmured, his mouth moving against her knuckles. "Anymore than I could harm you—"

His lips found hers then, in a kiss so gentle, so tender, she couldn't summon even a little resistance. The hard, challenging man of a moment ago was gone, and in his place was a tender cavalier, a man who could be trusted to protect a woman under his care with the utmost vigilance.

She could feel his bare chest pressing against her breasts, the warmth of his hands on her back and her hips. His mouth lifted, and brushed her cheeks, her nose, the top of her forehead, only to wander lower to the shell of her ear, the tip of her earlobe.

Treacherous longings were beginning to rise within her. "Alex —"

"Hush," he murmured into her hair. "You were subjected to the first part of the therapy—but we haven't finished yet."

"The finish" was a wonderfully warm tender kiss. There was no demand, no force, no urgent passion. Yet his mouth was that of a lover, a lover who, perhaps, had already tasted consummation and was now caught in the lovely afterglow, the closeness that lingered. It was as if she had already given him that ultimate gift and he was confirming their love. Cathy melted against him, feeling sheltered and warm. Feeling amazingly complete and suddenly free somehow.

Much too soon, his mouth left hers. After another moment of holding her close, he said softly, "I'll take you home now."

He went back to the coffee table and picked up one of the scripts, his shirt hanging loosely around his body.

She asked huskily, "What are you doing?"

"You'll need this." He handed her the black-bound book.

She opened her mouth, but before she could voice her protest, he stopped her. "If you're truly worried about my reputation, you will have all four acts memorized by the first rehearsal on a week from Monday. Don't bother coming to *Cactus Flower* dress rehearsal tomorrow night. We'll manage without you."

Then, as he escorted her to the door he closed the trap. "Barbara was pleased when I told her I was sure you'd be able to take her place. She said she would feel much better about leaving the cast, knowing that you have the experience and skill to learn the role quickly."

On the opening night of *Cactus Flower,* she stood backstage watching the cast wait for Alex, and their first-night nerves were so vivid she nearly began to tremble with panic herself, although she had no reason to. Devlin Smith lit a cigarette under the NO SMOKING sign, something he never would have done in rehearsal. Larry muttered over a bank of lights that weren't working, and Barbara Stanton looked pale, shock-ridden. Cathy longed to go to her side and put her arm around the girl's shoulders, but she knew Barbara would be embarrassed if she did. She suppressed her own panic-driven nerves. Barbara's state of mind was crucial. Much of the play's appeal depended on her. If she was tense and afraid, even Pamela Field's charm wouldn't be enough to save the evening from disaster.

Alex had not yet arrived. Pamela seemed calm . . . but she had been in a frenzy only seconds ago because the silver star she habitually wore in her hair had been lost. It was Pamela's good-luck charm, and she was terrified to go on stage without it. Everyone searched frantically until Millie, the red-haired girl who did their hairstyles, found it under someone's purse.

Alex appeared on stage and stood in front of the curtain, and everyone's eyes were focused on him, as if he were the source of their confidence. He wore a summer suit of light blue and as he walked across the stage with that halting walk, Cathy felt her pulses beating against her skin.

When he reached the middle of the stage, there was a hushed, expectant silence. Then, just as Alex opened his mouth, Larry came out, carrying a high wooden stool, the kind a conductor in an orchestra might use. The seat of the stool was wrapped with brown paper. With a flourish, Larry presented the stool to Alex. "A little gift to show our appreciation—your director's chair."

Alex took the stool from Larry and swept an amused glance around the group. He pulled the paper off the seat, stood staring for a moment at it, and then threw back his head and laughed. Cathy pressed forward along with the rest of the cast to see the cause of Alex's amusement. To satisfy their curiosity, Alex held up the stool. Written across the wooden seat, in black Gothic letters were the words, *Reardon's rear here.* The cast burst into laughter. Alex put the stool on the floor, and with great ceremony hoisted himself to sit on it. "Now that all things are in their proper place—" There was another outburst of laughter. His eyes swept over the cast. "I want to thank you for this—" his hand swept downward, "and thank you, too, for your promptness and dedication during these five weeks." The amused smile faded from his lips and he said seriously, "Tonight you will recreate a play in the old and venerable tradition of the art. We all thrive on that heightened sense of awareness that good theater gives us. If we have done our job well, the audience comes away from the play feeling more alive. And so do we." He glanced around at each one of them and smiled again. Cathy knew that if she were one of the cast, she would feel that all the hours of rehearsals were well-repaid by that rare laughter earlier, and this lift of lips now—just an hour before curtain time. It was the highest accolade he could give them, the ultimate sign that he was confident they would do well. He went on to say as much. "I can feel your excitement, your energy, and enthusiasm. I know the audience will too."

He slid from the stool and carried it with him off the stage, and a nervous murmuring began at once. They knew they were dismissed. The stage emptied quickly and Cathy saw Larry beckon to Alex. He gave the young man his close attention, his head bent, listening. Minutes later, with Larry stationed at the control panel board, Alex stripped off his jacket and climbed the scaffolding with a replacement bulb in his hand.

Why did he do that, Cathy thought, her stomach clenching as he leaned over a rung of the ladder and reached out to the offending bulb? Any other director would have sent Larry up.

She watched, her heart in her mouth. Alex completed the change and came down the ladder. He looked at her, but before her eyes gave her away, she escaped out the exit door.

With his jacket back on, Alex looked cool and unperturbed as he slid into his seat beside her minutes before the play began. The dark theater was packed. The mayor was there as well as representatives from the *Chronicle* and the *Times-Union.* There had already been a leader story about Alex, his accident, and his work on the play. But if he felt an unusual tension, she couldn't see signs of it.

The curtain went up. There were appreciative murmurs when Devlin came on stage. The play opened with Barbara, as Toni, unconscious after trying to commit suicide. This gave Barbara a chance to ease into the role without facing the audience. Her first real acting came when she woke up and began to kiss Devlin back. This got the expected laugh, and Cathy could feel Alex relax.

As the play progressed, she found herself listening for the tell-tale coughing an audience did when it was bored. There was none, only laughter in all the right places. Barbara was doing well, blossoming into the part.

The audience reception to Pamela was electric. She was the star; she knew it, and they knew it. Alex however had directed the action skillfully, and the rest of the cast was more than just a foil for Pamela's talents. The show worked as a whole—because of Alex's conception.

At the end of the play, the loud applause and the standing ovation for Pamela brought a smile to Alex's lips. The actress called to him and asked him to come out for an impromptu bow. His appearance on the stage brought another wild round of clapping.

The cast party was to be at Alex's house, and Cathy was acting as hostess. When the clapping died away and the cast and Alex disappeared behind the blue velvet curtain, Cathy rose and slipped out of the theatre.

She drove to Alex's house and let herself in with the key he had given her. The soft drinks and liquors they had ordered that afternoon were chilling in the refrigerator. One by one, the cast began to arrive. She set out bottles and glasses and put the pizza in the oven to heat.

They began to arrive in noisy, elated confusion, still on an emotional high. Devlin turned on the stereo and James pushed the couch back to make a circle on the bare floor for dancing. Millie acted as bartender and dispensed the drinks. Barbara and her husband, a tall, well-built man, walked out on the floor and began to dance.

Cathy stood behind the snack bar, watching, her mind only aware of one thing—that Pamela and Alex had not yet arrived.

"I thought women were liberated these days, and didn't spend all their time in the kitchen." Devlin Smith leaned over the counter and smiled into her face. "Why don't you come out and dance with me?"

"Why don't I?" she asked easily, and walked round the snack bar to step into his arms.

He was young and virile and handsome and his grip was firm. It amused her to think that what he had learned from Alex on stage he was applying to her. She should have enjoyed dancing with him—if that was what it could be called. They had very little room; Devlin was forced to confine his movements to small steps in the same place.

"Quarter for them."

"What?" She lifted her head to look at him.

"Hasn't the price of thoughts gone up like everything else?"

She smiled. "I doubt if they're worth a quarter."

He moved with her in his arms and then said, "Was I okay tonight?"

"You were very good, Devlin," she said, smiling at his anxious need for reassurance, "every one was. There'll be nothing but raves in the papers tomorrow."

"Now all we have to do is repeat it for five more nights."

She laughed softly. "You're beginning to sound just like a New York professional."

He gave her a shrewd look. "Speaking of professionals—rumor has it Barbara's leaving—and you're taking her place."

She was silent for a moment and then said lightly, "Strange the things you hear."

"Is it true?" he persisted.

Intent on distracting him with an amusing reply, she was smiling up into Devlin's face . . . when Alex Reardon with Pamela on his arm walked into the room. The intent green gaze came zinging at her, flickered briefly over her hand still on Devlin's neck—and moved away.

"Hello, everybody, we're here." Pamela's arm was linked in Alex's and her face was radiant with triumph. "We've just finishing talking to the press." Capturing the attention of everyone, she smiled up into Alex's face. "Not the reviewers—some staff reporters that wanted to cover the entire story of the company more in depth. In a day or two, everyone in the area will know about us." She signaled the end of her announcement by slipping out of her white ruffled stole and handing it to Alex. The dress she wore was stunning, a brilliant blue silk that left her shoulders bare. "Would you get me a drink, darling? Make it on the light side."

The music stopped and the couples urged Devlin to put on another tape. Dragging her by the hand, he made his way through the crush of bodies to the stereo.

The party went on to the early hours without showing signs of abating. She danced with Devlin again and with James. From his arms she watched Alex moving around the floor with Pamela, his hand splayed against her waist.

Involuntarily she flinched and James felt it at once. "Is something wrong?"

"I think I need a breath of air. Do you mind?"

"I'll come with you—"

"No, you stay with your Anne. I'll be fine."

She seized the opportunity to escape. Glad that she had driven her own car, she snatched up her purse and went out the door.

The dark enclosed her in silent warmth. Very soon, the sun would be coming up. She was breathing a sigh of thankfulness that she hadn't been blocked by other cars when a sound in the silence made her whirl around in shocked surprise.

"Where are you going?"

Alex's voice. Her heart beat furiously against her breast. The angry words that rolled in her mind refused to come out. She stared at him, watching him emerge out of the darkness, his face a dark shadow above the pale blue silk of his shirt.

"Home," she said. "I'm tired."

"Too much dancing?"

The soft, sardonic words goaded her into replying, "Yes, that must be it."

"Not too long ago," he said softly, "you proposed a toast to the success of this night. Now at my moment of triumph," the words were softly mocking, "you're running away."

"You have—others to share your triumph with you."

"But I want you . . . to share it with me."

His voice lingered like a seductive murmur on the summer air and an aching warmth filled her.

"Alex, please, I really must go. I'm tired and I—"

He took a step forward. A wisp of a breeze swirled the skirt of her black silk dress out against the fine wool of his trousers. "Don't think you can escape with such platitudes. You and I have gone far beyond that."

He lifted his hand and touched her cheekbone. "You know I want you." His lightly caressing fingers made her face tingle with pleasure. He explored the smoothly-textured cheek, traced around her chin and then dropped his hand to the soft vulnerable base of her throat.

"Alex . . ."

His name was a sigh in the night, a half-protesting, half-pleading sound. He bent his head to breathe in the scent of her.

"You can't say it, can you? You can't admit that you want me as much as I want you. . . ."

She clutched his shoulders and fought for control. "Alex . . . please don't. I can't—"

Abruptly, he let go of her and stepped away. A chill touched her skin. "Stop playing games, Cathy." His words came in a harsh whisper. "Admit you want me."

She fought to keep her eager body from gliding into his arms. "It's true there's an attraction between us—"

He cursed softly. "You can't even be honest with yourself, can you?"

Desperately groping, she said, "We're going to be working together—"

He made a contemptuous sound in his throat. "We're adults—and professionals. Whatever happens between us doesn't have to affect our work."

"But it will—"

He was silent in the darkness for a long, intolerable moment. On a harsh intake of breath, he spoke. "I've been wrong about you from the first, haven't I?" The subtle menace in his voice alarmed her. He took a step closer and she had to brace herself not to back away.

"You've been leading me on with your sweet reluctance—until you got what you were after—a role in the play."

Every cell in her body felt pain, as if he were whipping her with his voice.

"I must say you were more clever than most," he went on relentlessly. "You fooled me completely. Congratulations."

"You can't really believe that," she said huskily.

"Is that what happened with Warren? Did you come on to him, charm him, entice him till he could hardly think straight and then refuse to deliver the goods?"

"That question doesn't deserve an answer." Numbed by his attack, her blood chilled, she put a hand on her car to steady herself. He moved like lightning, clasping her hand and pulling her roughly against him. "You're not going anywhere until you've heard what I have to say."

She lifted her head, and held so close to him, even in the darkness, she could see his face. His eyes burned into hers. She stiffened her back and met them with her chin up and a fire in her own violet depths. "Then get on with it," she said defiantly, refusing to be cowed. "I'd like to go home sometime tonight."

His grip involuntarily tightened on her. A quaking shudder of anger went through him. Then he loosened his hands and stepped away. "Go home. Run away. But I'm warning you—if there is a way to get to you—I'll find it."

He pivoted and disappeared into the night. She waited, afraid to breathe, feeling like a small bird of prey hiding in the bush until the predator passes.

Her acute senses had not been wrong. Alex turned suddenly. "I'll pick you up around eight-thirty Sunday night."

She stared back at him. Perspiration made her palms clammy. "For the dance? But I thought—"

Crickets sang into the silence. Then his low voice said, "What did you think?"

"I thought—you'd be going with Pamela."

"No," he said, the menacing sound of satisfaction in his voice. "She's going with James. You, Miss Taylor, are going with me."

He turned round again, his back rigid. He covered the small distance down the hill to the cottage in record time, it seemed to her. When he pulled open the door of the house, light and laughter spilled out. Then the door closed, and she sagged against the car, no longer able to stand by her own effort.

CHAPTER EIGHT

She walked down the stairs, concentrating on the clock. An old familiar friend, it seemed to be the one thing she remembered from childhood. The sound of its constant ticking and deep, lovely chimes had always been reassuring. If she concentrated on the ticking, she could block out the sound of Alex's deep, attractive voice coming from inside the living room, and try to accept with a measure of calm the fact that tonight she would be riding with him in the back seat of her father's Mercedes-Benz to the country club.

Audrey had insisted that they all go together; Cathy wasn't sure why. She hesitated on the bottom step, her hand on the polished wood of the railing. She tried all the little tricks to rid herself of nervousness, taking a deep breath to relax the breathing muscles, and concentrating on the thought of a still, quiet pool of water. The techniques helped, and she stepped down to the parquet floor. Her high-heeled sandals made a little click, and there was a sudden silence beyond the double doors. She looked into the room. Alex was standing behind the couch, holding a glass in his hand. He turned to look at her and for a moment, she thought he didn't recognize her. There was a fleeting emotion she couldn't identify in his gaze and then a dark, closed look fell over his face and his smoky lashes dropped, half-shadowing his eyes. His cool look was like a frosty wind touching her skin.

"How lovely you look, Cathy." Audrey put down her glass and came toward her, the long burgundy silk gown she wore rustling as she walked. "Alex will be the envy of every man there."

Alex's expression was bland. "I certainly will."

She felt the color come into her face. Something about her gown obviously displeased him. She couldn't think why. She had chosen her dress with great care. It was a creamy voile with a long flowing skirt, tucked to fit tightly around her breasts and waist. The dress was all the more provocative because it bared every inch of her throat and shoulders and yet had long, dropped sleeves that covered her arms from above her elbows to the ruffles at her wrists. She had piled her hair on top of her head, a few wispy tendrils framing her face, softening the style. She wore no jewelry.

"Jason, dear, come look at Cathy. Did you realize what a gorgeous daughter you have?"

Something quivered along her nerve ends. Every particle of her seemed to be aware of Alex's watchful stillness. Her father straightened away from the mantel, gave Cathy a fleeting look, and leaned forward to set his glass on the low table in front of the couch. "Yes, I did." His eyes flickered over her for another brief glance. "You look charming, Cathy, well worth waiting for." He turned to Audrey. "Are we ready, my dear?"

Audrey cast Cathy a quick, concerned look. Cathy lifted her head and smiled a bright, brittle smile. Audrey murmured her agreement that they were ready and picked up the matching shawl of burgundy silk from a corner of the couch. There were good-byes to Melissa and Danielle, both standing in the hall and looking at the formally attired people with two entirely different expressions; a gleam of satisfaction shone in Melissa's eyes, while Danielle's were bright with longing.

In the car there was room enough for her to settle into the corner, a safe distance away from Alex. Audrey kept the conversation going, telling Alex something of the local people he would be meeting. His answers were conversational but brief.

At the club, she climbed out of the car. The night was alive with summer sounds, the scent of honeysuckle heavy in the air.

Alex escorted her up the five steps silently, his hand on her elbow.

Inside, the room was full of circular tables, already half-filled with people. Waitresses in black dresses carried trays to and fro, and a band was playing soft music to the side of a smooth circular dance floor. On each of the tables, a white tablecloth gleamed under the flame of a candle that flickered in a curved blue glass bowl.

Audrey led the way to a table set amid the others. Jason Taylor pulled the cushioned leather chair out for his wife, and Alex did the same for Cathy. She managed to sit down without touching him. He bent to fit his tall, lean body into the chair, stretching his legs out. His jacket, a formal white, fell away from his lean waist. He wore a pearl gray cummerbund over his dark trousers and somehow, Cathy's eyes seemed to focus on the tiny pearl buttons just above it that held his shirt closed.

The waitress came, and drinks were ordered. She sat, her face cool, her mind on tenterhooks. *Alex,* her mind whispered. *Alex.* He was interfering with her thought processes awake or asleep. She had dreamt about him last night. The strange thing about the dream was that it wasn't bizarre or unreal at all. In the dream he had told her he loved her. And she had felt a blaze of elation well up inside her that she could still remember, the feeling vivid and real to her still.

But this wasn't a dream, this was reality. And though the man seated next to her had made no secret of his desire for her, somehow she knew with a razor-sharp pain that he would never tell her he loved her.

The drinks came and he took his from the waitress and lowered it to the table. His hands were sensitive, lean, and finely molded. Just looking at their taut strength disturbed her.

She averted her eyes and lifted her own glass to her lips. She had ordered a light, dry wine and she sipped it now, grateful for its cool tartness.

She was just placing the glass on the table when she saw James and Pamela enter the room. Pamela was exquisite in a light blue clinging silk that wrapped itself lovingly around her neck and body. She stood looking about the room eagerly and when her eyes found Alex, her lips lifted in a smile. She gestured toward them and James nodded.

Pamela's brittle gaiety spilled over them. "Hello, everyone. May we join you?"

Permission was given, and chairs were gathered from another table. They crowded closer to make room, and Cathy felt the brush of Alex's knee against her own.

It was a subtle kind of torture, being so close to him and yet so far. The torture became supremely more refined when Pamela sat down next to him and captured his attention immediately with light, amusing conversation. She seemed always to be touching him as she talked, her fingertips brushing his sleeve, her shoulder against his. Cathy gazed out over the dance floor, wishing desperately that she were home during a silence broken only by the ticking of the clock. She fastened her eyes at a point beyond her Audrey's shoulder and called on everything she had ever learned as an actress to look poised and cool.

As a result she was the first one to see Barbara, lovely in a pale green silk gown, walk away from a tall, well-built man, and head for their table.

"Alex, Mrs. Meriweather was looking for you. She wants to start the progressive dance with you as her partner."

"You see, darling?" Pamela drawled. "The Meriweather woman is absolutely champing at the bit to dance with you."

Alex rose and glanced round the table. "Excuse me, won't you? Duty calls."

Pamela watched Alex walk away with Barbara, a contemplative look on her face, her fingers caressing the stem of her wine glass. "Barbara was telling me the director who did the summer shows last year was short and a bit on the bald side. The progressive dance only lasted a minute or two." She sipped her wine and put her glass on the table, her lips lifted in a smile. "Somehow I have a feeling it's going to last much longer this year," she said softly, turning her head to watch Alex lead a short, dark-haired woman to the floor.

The dance began, and Alex circled alone with the woman, holding her at just the right distance, not too close and not too far away. There was no sign of his injury. He danced without any evidence of his peculiar, arhythmic walk.

"He has absolutely no self-consciousness about his injured leg," Pamela murmured. "Strange, isn't it? That accident could have left him crushed and bitter, but it didn't. It made him stronger, I think. His directing has more depth and power now than it ever had. He'll be bigger than he was before."

"Do you think so?" Audrey asked thoughtfully. "I thought I noticed a certain—distracted quality about him lately. But—perhaps it's my imagination."

The music stopped. Alex bowed his head to the woman and released her with just the right amount of reluctance. He returned to the table to stand beside Audrey. "I hope you have no objection, Jason, if I dance with your wife?"

Cathy's father gave his hearty permission. The dancing continued until the music stopped. An elderly man, his face beaming with happiness, approached Cathy. "Jason, I've been waiting for this chance to claim your lovely daughter, if I may."

"That's her decision, I'm sure," her father said with a slight smile. "Cathy, this is William Bronson, an—old friend."

William Bronson was just slightly shorter than she and wore a red carnation in his buttonhole that signified he was on the board of directors of the theater.

He took her into his arms and said, "This is such a delightful occasion. Our one chance to mingle with the stars, so to speak."

"I'm afraid I don't quite fall in that category—"

"Ah, but I'm sure you will, Ms. Taylor. Mr. Reardon has spoken very highly of you to the board. I believe he intends to announce your acceptance of the part of Hedvig tonight."

"You must be mistaken."

The little man drew back. "I assure you I'm not. He was quite adamant about it."

"It doesn't seem necessary. . . ."

"Not necessary, perhaps, but politic. Mr. Reardon is a clever man. He knows how much the public loves a Cinderella story. Have you known Mr. Reardon long?"

"Not too long . . ." The music stopped, and she couldn't stifle the quick sense of relief she felt. William Bronson released her reluctantly and went in search of a new partner. A quick glance at their table told her her father was the only occupant. She waited, and when she saw that Audrey was dancing with the young lawyer who had been at her father's house that first evening, she walked slowly over to the table.

"Would you care to dance with me, Father?"

From the expression on his face, he patently wouldn't, but he got to his feet. When they were on the floor, she stepped into his arms, aware that he was looking about the room for Audrey. She stiffened. "Father, if you'd really rather not, there's no reason to—"

"What?" He looked down at her as if he were surprised to see her in front of him.

"Never mind." Stoically, she closed her mouth, and he continued to moved around the floor with her with a bored indifference.

"In that dress you look exactly like your mother," he said abruptly. Stunned, she made a misstep and he had to catch her. She couldn't believe it. He had never spoken of her mother to her. As a child there had been an impenetrable wall of silence facing her whenever she had asked him about her mother. "I do?"

"Yes," he said coolly. "We were going to a charity ball in Rochester, and I didn't know her very well yet. I'd only seen her once before. But that night, I was as bowled over by sight of her . . . just as Alex Reardon was by you."

"He wasn't . . ."

"Nonsense. Of course he was. Are you in love with him?"

She averted her eyes. "Am I on the witness stand?"

"I think I'd like the truth," he countered softly. "Anything else is a waste of time."

"Why should it matter to you?"

He drew back in surprise. "Because I'm your father."

She bit back a sharp denial of that fact. "Let's just say the jury's still out," she replied with a lightness she didn't feel.

"And that's my answer," he said curtly, "a flip backhand combined with a subtle slap at my profession?" They circled in angry silence. "I don't know why I should be surprised," he muttered. "That's all I've ever gotten from you when I've expressed an interest in your life. Somehow, I imagined that you were past the rebellious stage."

If he had suddenly stopped and turned her over his knee in the middle of the floor, she couldn't have been more shocked. Had he expressed an interest in her life and been given flip answers that hurt him so much he was reluctant to ask again? Her mind whirling, she tried to recall specific incidents. One came back in vivid detail. The night she had thrown the china cat through the window.

She had done it because of a boy, of course, a special boy who had chosen another girl to spend his summer afternoon on the lake with. And when her father had asked her why she had thrown the cat through the window, she had not wanted to admit the truth. He was a cold man she hardly knew, and she couldn't confess to him she was in the throes of her first crush on a member of the opposite sex. So, instead, she had shrugged her shoulders and replied with all the insouciance of a thirteen-year-old, "Because I didn't want it. It's silly and childish, and I wasn't a child anymore."

And her father, totally ignorant of the agonies of adolescent females, and unable to see the immaturity under the bravado, turned a deaf ear to her cry for understanding and reacted with a cold anger that raised the wall between them even higher.

The music ended and her father escorted her back to the table. The evening went on. She drank and talked and laughed, but she couldn't have said a moment later what any of it was about.

She desperately needed time alone to think, but it wasn't to be. The band had disappeared, and Alex had risen and was mounting the small stage. After a moment or two of fiddling with the microphone, he began to introduce the members of the cast and the production staff, asking them to stand as he announced their names. He did it smoothly and well, telling two personal anecdotes about amusing things that had happened during rehearsal. By the end of the introductions, he had played on the crowd's sense of humor like a master, bringing about a thoroughly relaxed, receptive atmosphere with their laughter. He paused for a moment and then went off to the side and reappeared with the long white box of roses that Cathy had purchased for the occasion. He presented them to Mrs. Meriweather with an appropriate speech, thanking her for her dedication to the Community Theater. The woman blushed and was almost pretty as she smiled into Alex's face.

When the speeches were nearly over, there was a little silence. Alex stepped to the microphone again.

"Some of you may have already heard that Barbara Stanton is leaving the cast of *The Wild Duck*. We've been most fortunate to find a talented replacement for her right in our midst. Cathy Taylor has been working as my assistant, and she has had extensive experience in both the theater and the cinema. I'd like to take this opportunity to recognize Cathy and to thank her publicly for stepping into a difficult role at such a late hour."

He insisted that she stand. She did, only because she had no choice, but her smile was wooden. There was a murmur throughout the room and then a polite round of applause.

When Alex came back to the table, Audrey leaned across and touched Cathy's hand. "I'm so glad. I knew something good would happen for you when you met Alex. Congratulations, Cathy."

"Thank you," she said with a husky catch in her voice.

"I didn't know you were going to be our new Hedvig." There was cool appraisal in Pamela's eyes. "Are you sure you're up to it? It is a rather—classic role."

She met Pamela's eyes straight on. "No, I'm not sure I'm up to it," she answered coolly. "I'll simply do the very best I can. That's all anyone can do."

Pamela leaned back in her chair and the silver star in her bright blond hair caught a gleam of light. "Believe me, dear, Alex will want that—and then some. Or are you prepared to make an exception in her case, darling?"

"You know I never make exceptions, Pam," he said softly.

From somewhere behind her a voice said, "Good evening." She recognized Devlin's smooth tones and caught a glimpse of him out of her peripheral vision as he came to stand beside her, his hand on the back of her chair. "I'm Devlin Smith, sir," he said, extending his hand toward Jason Taylor. Cathy's father took his hand, a puzzled frown creasing his brows. "Arthur Smith's boy?"

"No, he is my uncle. My father's name is Theodore." He turned to Cathy, as if he had performed the necessary preliminaries. "Will you dance with me?"

She could think of no real reason to refuse him. "Yes, of course."

Alex moved in his chair, and a sudden, almost electric sensation of danger sizzled along her nerve ends. Sitting beside Alex in a darkened rehearsal hall for weeks had made her increasingly aware that while she couldn't read his face to discover what he was feeling, she could read his body with unerring accuracy. She knew the danger signs well, an impatient tug at the crease of his trousers, a thinning of his lips, a slight leaning to one side with a hand on his temple, and worst of all, a sudden forward movement in his chair.

Conscious of his displeasure, she rose and allowed Devlin to press her toward the dance floor, a possessive hand at her back. Pamela's bright voice seemed to echo after them. "This song is rather nice, Alex. Why don't you ask me to dance?"

Even though she was walking away, she could hear the soft answer delivered in that familiar, sardonic tone. "Would you care to dance, Pamela?"

"I'd be delighted."

Devlin turned her. As he pulled her close, she gazed over his shoulder—and saw that Alex and Pamela had followed almost on their heels, and that Alex was watching her move into Devlin's arms. His eyes glittered, and there was a grim tightness about his mouth. Then his lips relaxed, and he turned his back to her and reached for Pamela, folding her into his arms with that same male assurance and mastery that he had demonstrated that night on stage.

They revolved out of her vision. The music was soft and slow and she followed Devlin in silent misery, her thoughts on Alex. The lights were very dim now, and gradually she became aware of the way Devlin was holding her, the subtle sexual messages he was sending. Unbidden, the thought came to her that never again would any other man but Alex elicit a response from her body . . . or her mind.

With every slow turning step, Devlin's leg insinuated itself between hers. She felt only a faint impatience. She moved slightly, trying to create a distance between herself and Devlin.

He pulled her closer. Imperceptibly, she leaned back, creating an easing of the pressure of his body against hers.

"I just don't turn you on at all, do I?" He let her move away and look up into his face.

"Are you supposed to?"

"Well, let's just say I—kind of hoped I would. But I can't get through to you at all, can I? Your line is busy."

"And your line is a little tired," she said dryly.

"It's not a line," he said flatly, and pulled her close again. "Come out on the terrace with me." His mouth lingered at her temple and she knew he was aroused. His heart beat heavily against hers and the hand that held hers was warm.

"Devlin, I'm with Alex—"

"Don't try to put me off with that one, Cathy. Just level with me and admit that Reardon's got you tied up in a neat little package."

"He hasn't—"

"Hasn't he? He put you in Barbara's slot without the flicker of an eyelash." He was silent for a moment as they turned around the floor and Cathy felt the heat rising in her face and her body stiffen with tension.

"I do have some experience—"

"On the stage?" Devlin asked coolly. "Or in his bedroom?"

Furious, she thrust him away. "You know there's something you really ought to learn," she said in a low, angry tone.

"Whatever you want to teach me, honey," he said, pulling her close again, "I'm willing to learn."

"Including how to take no for an answer?" she shot back.

"Hey, don't get sore. I was only kidding around—"

She felt as if the top of her head was going to fly off. The room was stifling. The heat combined with the cigarette smoke, and heavy scent of perfume sent her walking swiftly to the tall doors that led out to the terrace. She opened one and escaped into the cool darkness. There was a noise behind her, and she held her breath, but no footsteps came after her. She was alone.

She pressed her hands against her hot cheeks and ran down the steps that led to a grassy expanse where round flower beds had been carefully tended. She walked along a path, into the shadow of tall trees, away from the lights streaming from the windows. A few feet away from the path she discovered a stone bench and she sank down in the shadowed coolness and curled her hands around its cold edges . . .

The sound of a step made her heart leap. She wasn't safe, after all. Devlin had followed her. She steeled herself and rose to face him. She wouldn't run, not this time. But it was Alex's white jacket that gleamed in the moonlight in front of her.

"What happened?" His words were harsh and clipped.

"Nothing."

"Smith said something to upset you—what was it?"

"Nothing, really."

He took a step and came closer. "If I have to go back in there and choke the truth out of him, I will."

She stood silent and he turned on his heel.

"He thinks we're having an affair." The words were husky, barely audible, but they halted him. He turned.

"And that upset you so much you came running out here like a frightened rabbit?"

She shook her head.

"No, it's something more than that isn't it?" he guessed astutely.

She stood watching him, knowing that the keen mind was working at a furious rate.

"Let's see," he said with a cool thoughtfulness. "I think I can recreate the scenario without too much trouble. He makes a pass at you, you rebuff him. He accuses you of sleeping with me and then suggests that's why you were chosen to replace Barbara."

Her anguished face gave him his answer. He swore softly. "That young self-righteous swine." His hands were clenching ominously at his sides and his face was pale with fury.

"Please—just—forget it."

He took a step closer. "Nothing he says matters to me. But what about you?"

"I'll forget it, too," she promised huskily.

He held out his hand. "Then don't give him the satisfaction of knowing you're out here hiding in the dark. Come in with me."

She remembered the way she had felt just watching that hand lift his glass to his lips. But she couldn't refuse to place her hand in his.

The moment she touched him, she knew it was a mistake. He must have felt her whole body tremble. His own cool control seemed to shatter. He pulled her roughly into his arms, and his voice was a husky rasp in her ear. "I was a fool to let him get near you. Every time he does, he hurts you. . . ."

"Alex, you're not my keeper. . . ."

"I'd like to be," he muttered, "the way you look tonight, I'd like to lock you away for a hundred years. . . ."

He bent his head and took her mouth, his hands warm and intimate on her back. For a moment, she kept her mouth closed and refused to accept the probing caress of his tongue. He lifted his head just enough to murmur, "Don't, honey. Let me kiss you the way you deserve to be kissed—now, when you need it."

His lips returned to entreat and tantalize, and when she could no longer hold her own longings at bay, his tongue flickered past the barrier of her teeth and found the sweetness it sought. His mouth and hands worked their persuasive magic on her body, while his tongue touched sensitive places in her mouth she hadn't known existed.

Under the light shirring of her dress, she could feel the beat of his heart against her, the disturbed tempo of his breathing. His warm palms kneaded her bare shoulders gently, imitating the circular movements of his tongue inside her mouth.

Her hands found their way under his jacket easily, to the hard muscled flesh beneath the fabric of his shirt.

"Yes, Cathy, yes. Touch me. Hold me. . . ."

As if to stop his own cry of need, he buried his mouth against her neck. When she thought she would drown in the pleasure of his roving mouth as it wandered along the top of her gown, he lifted his head and murmured into her hair, "He's right about one thing. I do want you."

The empty ache inside her begged her to tell him the truth, that she wanted him just as desperately. But she was afraid. Afraid and wary. She had loved Wade . . . and he had left her without a second thought. And Wade had asked her to marry him. He had told her he loved her repeatedly. No word of love had ever crossed Alex's lips. He wanted her . . . but he didn't love her.

She pushed at him. "Alex . . . let me go."

His hands fell away from her. She couldn't see his face in the moonlight, but the movement of the silk shirt told her he was breathing rapidly and fighting for control. Waves of tension flowed in the night air between them. At last he said in a low voice, "Will you come inside with me?"

She was silent for a fraction of a second, still fighting down the strong urge to move into his arms and cry out the love words she ached to say to him. "Yes, of course."

Inside, the band was playing and there was movement and confusion near the terrace doors so that their entrance went unnoticed except by those few standing close by. Cathy threaded her way to the table where her father and Audrey sat, fighting down her awareness of the man behind her, knowing that her lips were swollen by the warmth of his kiss, feeling the light touch of his hand on her waist.

Alex pulled out her chair and she sat down, not looking at him. Pamela and James had left the table and were dancing, but curiosity danced in Audrey's eyes. Her father's face was unreadable. He might have been in court.

"There you are, you two." Audrey's voice was cheerful. "Cathy, would you like some more wine?"

"Yes," she said, feeling the need of something cooling to ease the heat of Alex's kiss.

The waiter appeared within minutes with their drinks. Cathy sipped hers, wishing the alcohol could give her instant oblivion.

The wine tasted delicious. She kept the delicate crystal under her fingers and watched Pamela return to the table on James's arm.

The evening ground on, with Pamela engaging Alex's attention. He seemed content to listen to her flattering comments. What his feelings were about her hand tracing circles on the white jacket of his sleeve was difficult to tell.

The waiter came around again, and Cathy ordered more wine. It went down much too easily and she had to signal the steward and tell him of her desire for more.

She suddenly realized she was feeling much better. She must be. She seemed to be laughing with Audrey about nothing at all.

Alex leaned forward. "I'm sorry to break this up, but Cathy promised me a dance."

Had she? She couldn't remember. His steady unrelenting gaze told her she had, and he would see to it that she kept her promise.

She got up and felt an instant lightheadedness. That would pass when she was out on the floor, she was sure.

She walked to the dance floor and turned, conscious of a tingling anticipation before Alex took her into his arms.

He pulled her roughly against him and she relaxed, satisfied, and, with a wanton boldness, slid both her hands up over the smooth lapel of his jacket to circle his neck. He had little recourse but to clasp her around the waist and slide his hands to an intimate position at the back of her hips. She pressed against him. His instant tension gave her a perverse pleasure. He wasn't indifferent to her touch; even though he fought his response, he couldn't hide it.

She lay languorously in his arms, her head against his shoulder, her feet moving to match his movements. His voice was a smooth stone thrown in her pool of thoughts. "Has it occurred to you that you've had too much to drink?"

"Yes, it has." She lifted her head and gazed up into his face. "But I disregarded the thought. After all, this is my night to celebrate."

"Is it?" He lifted a dark eyebrow. "Do you see yourself as an instant star?"

"Yes," she said unguardedly, "an instant overnight success. After four years of drama school, two years in repertory, two films and eight plays on off-Broadway—I deserve to be an overnight success, don't you think?"

His mouth twitched. "I think the wine has gone to your head."

She shrugged. "So be it. It's so pleasant to forget sometimes, Alex. Don't you ever want to just forget?"

"Hush," he said with soft indulgence.

She lifted her head. "My emotions are showing, Alex. Isn't that what you wanted?"

There was a silence as he gazed into her face. "Yes," he replied bluntly. "But now is hardly the time or place."

"No," she said sadly. "It's never the time or place."

She laid her head on his chest, thinking how sad life was. What a pity he didn't love her. She loved him so much. She let her fingertips rub the indentation at his neck, brushing the little hairs the wrong way.

Something seemed to be bothering him. His body was hard with tension. Abruptly, he broke away from her and led her across the dance floor and back to the table. She had made him angry, she supposed. She stood passively beside him, his grip on her arm allowing her to do little else.

Alex said something to her father that she didn't quite follow and Jason Taylor reached in his pocket and brought out his keys.

"Where are we going?" she asked insistently, as he towed her out of the crowded room and into the hallway.

"I'm taking you home," he answered shortly.

She tugged at his arm. "I don't want to go home. I'm celebrating. . . ."

He pushed her with a gentle firmness through the door and out into the warm night. She protested, but her protestations had no effect on their forward movement across the parking lot.

When he had installed her in the front seat of the car and slid in under the wheel, she turned on him. "Would you stop treating me like a child?"

"With pleasure," he replied succinctly. "As soon as you stop acting like one." He started the car with controlled skill, and since he had not turned on the air conditioning, she rolled down the window. The breeze on her face brought back a touch of sanity—and with it—pain. For an entire lifetime, she had been cut off from her father because of pride. The empty years had not been what he wanted either. They had just . . . happened. They both had had too much pride to try to bridge the chasm between them.

No, that wasn't the exact truth either. Her father had tried. She was the one who had rejected him.

In a weary effort to try to stop the grinding thoughts, she put a hand to her forehead.

"Most people don't have their hangovers till morning." Alex's voice mocked her softly.

The need to protect herself made her answer in a light, determined tone, "I've never done the conventional thing, why start now?"

"No, you haven't, have you?"

He said the words with a careless expertise that was his stock in trade, but she knew he was referring to her marriage to Wade. She lapsed into silence, her nerves raw with pain.

After he had guided the car smoothly round the turn and into the driveway of her father's house, he killed the engine and turned in his seat. It was dark in the car and she couldn't see his face, only the outline of his head. She could see his jacket though; the whiteness of it caught fragments of light from the coach lamps that shone at the front of the house.

The dark night seemed to enclose them. She felt ragged and raw and utterly alone. She was empty inside, torn apart by an aching longing to have him reach out and pull her close to him. But he didn't. He simply sat and looked at her and saw—what? She didn't have the faintest idea.

So she asked him. "What do you see, Alex?"

"I see a woman who needs to go to bed." His voice had a harsh edge.

It was the perfect cue, and she didn't hesitate. Her voice a low, provocative sound, she asked, "With you?"

He leaned back in the seat. "No. I prefer my women sober."

"Then take me home with you," she said, reaching out and laying her hand on his lapel. "I'll be sober by morning." She trailed her hand down the placket of his shirt to the pearl stud in the middle of his chest.

"Stop it," he ordered sharply. "The role of seductress doesn't suit you."

She didn't take her hand away. "I thought I was playing it rather well." Her fingers separated the layers of silk and pulled the stud free. The back of it slipped through her fingers. "I've always thought I needed more variety in my roles. Is this how these things work? I've been wondering all evening."

He didn't touch her, but his voice had the harsh rasp of steel. "Cathy, I'm warning you . . ."

Another stud fell away. "Why are you resisting, Alex? Wouldn't you like your reward for being my knight in shining armor and saving me from Devlin?"

"What I'd like most," he enunciated each word with ominous clarity, "is to wring your beautiful neck."

"Then do it," she challenged him recklessly, turning the tables on him, repeating his words of that night she had never forgotten. "Put your hands around my neck and do it, Alex."

She reached for his hands and placed them around her bare throat. Under her palms, his hands tightened involuntarily on her smooth skin. She gazed back into the dark face and didn't flinch.

He was close enough now so she could see the glittering green of his eyes. "Someday, my sweet little repressed wildcat, you're going to push me too far."

"And what will happen then, dear, esteemed director?"

"I'll make love to you till you beg for mercy," he muttered in a husky rasp totally unlike him. His hands tightened and he bent his head and kissed her. She felt the cords in her neck move against his lean fingers as she strained to get closer to him and he resisted her efforts.

His mouth and grip gentled. His hands splayed out, touching the naked skin above her breasts. His shackling grip hadn't had the power over her that his gentle kiss and caress was having now. The nerves in her body seemed to leap and gather to pulse under the warm strength of his fingers.

She slid her hands under his jacket. Here in his arms, she was safe from the pain of her thoughts and the loneliness. When he ended the kiss without deepening it, she felt deprived. She wanted more. "Alex, take me home with you, please."

He broke away from her at once, and she bitterly regretted that her words had shattered the spell. "You're not going anywhere but upstairs to your own bed."

With a vicious tug at the door handle, he opened the car door and stepped out. She sat quiet, but mutinous. She didn't want to leave him. She wouldn't leave. She would simply sit in the car. He opened the door.

"I'm not going in," she told him. "I'm going with you."

He made a low, unintelligible sound that might have been a curse, reached in and lifted her in his arms.

"What are you doing? Put me down. I'm going with you."

He dragged her out of the car, shoved the door shut with his foot and climbed the steps of the porch to the door, depositing her on her feet beside it like a bundle of laundry. He pulled her father's keys from his pocket and after a moment, managed to open the door. When he saw she wasn't going to walk inside of her own free will, he hauled her up into his arms again. "Turn on the lights."

She did as she was told. He strode to the stairway and it was then she became aware of his uneven step.

"Put me down, Alex. I can walk."

"Be still." He tightened his hold on her and began to climb the stairs. He went unerringly to her bedroom and after she turned on the light switch there, he walked to the bed and dumped her unceremoniously into its soft depths.

In the bright light, sober reality intruded. She stared up at him. His chest was heaving slightly with his exertion, his eyes bright with angry mockery.

She shook her head, trying to collect her dazed thoughts. What had she been thinking of, openly offering herself to him after the wine had swept her inhibitions away? Suppose he had taken her up on her offer? Most other men would have—without the slightest compunction.

"Alex. Dear God. Alex, I'm sorry."

Something came and went in his eyes, she wasn't sure what. Compassion, perhaps. She couldn't bear the thought that he might be pitying her.

He stood staring down at her. The room seemed to reel with

the silence. Then he said softly, "Don't apologize. You'll pay me back one day—you can be sure of that." He stared down at her for a moment longer, then turned on his heel and went out of the room, his hand flicking the light switch off, leaving her in darkness.

CHAPTER NINE

The next Monday night, she dressed for her first rehearsal, alternating between defiant courage and face-heating shame. The weather added to her ill humor. It was stifling and close, muggy with the threat of a thunderstorm. The theater would be unbearably warm. She took a tepid shower, put on her underthings, and pulled on a pair of brief shorts. She took a halter top from her drawer, a red cotton bit of material that snapped around her neck and tied in the middle of her back. She put it on, looked at herself in the mirror—and took it off. She tried on a long-sleeved blouse—and ripped it off. The halter was retrieved from the floor and she snapped and tied herself into it with a controlled fury.

Dear God, why? Why did she remember everything in such vivid detail? Weren't people supposed to forget the things they did under the influence of alcohol? She hadn't. She remembered every single thing she had said and done last Saturday night.

That Alex would remember was a foregone conclusion. It took little imagination to know what form his retribution would take. She had seen directors reduce actors and actresses to trembling, nerve-shattered shells in full view of the rest of the cast. Alex had used restraint on the others because they were amateurs. He would have no such compunction with her, she was a professional. She was supposed to be able to endure and perform well even if he decided to shred her into little pieces.

The drive to the theater seemed far too short. She forced her legs to carry her up the steps and into the theater. The long red carpet stretched before her, leading her eyes inexorably to Alex, who sat on his stool in the aisle, watching the cast go through a scene.

As if he recognized the sound of her steps, he turned. His eyes met hers.

She took the initiative and prayed that her voice would not tremble. "Hello, Alex."

His answer was cool and impersonal. "You're early. We're just finishing up the first act."

She strove for calm. Her acting ability had never had a more severe test. "That's all right. I'll—sit here and watch." She chose a seat in relative safety three rows behind him.

The action on the stage continued. She wasn't acquainted with either of the men who portrayed the characters of Werle and his son, but they were excellent actors. Alex let them go on unhindered by comments. The actors gathered emotional tension, building relentlessly to the end of the scene in which Gregers denounces his father in self-righteous indignation.

A hard knot of tension curled in her stomach. The actors were good and they had already had several weeks of rehearsal. Could she learn everything she needed to know quickly enough to keep from dragging the whole production to a lower level?

The first act ended and Larry shifted the scenery quickly. It was her turn to walk up on stage and submit her skills to Alex's keen eyes and mind. She climbed the steps, her heart pounding. She had memorized her lines, but at this moment, she couldn't remember a word of them.

Pamela was playing Gina. She delivered her first line, calling Hedvig's name. Alex didn't like it. They had a prolonged discussion, one in which Alex urged her to search her memory for a time when she had called a young child in from play.

"Darling, you know I don't even like young children."

"Perhaps because you had six brothers and sisters," Alex replied softly, astounding Cathy. "Don't you remember calling them in to dinner?"

"We were too poor to eat," Pamela retorted, a smile on her lips.

"Pam, don't be obstructive. Try it again."

The actress did, and Alex seemed to be satisfied.

After Gina repeated her name, she was to answer. She said her line . . . and Alex stopped her.

"Cathy, I know this may be difficult for you, since you didn't have a mother, but there is a bond, a relationship between a mother and a child that is evident in everything the child says or does when she speaks to her mother. If you watch children, there is a subtle change in their faces and voices when they speak to their parents. Have you ever watched Danielle talking to Audrey? There's something there—an indefinable thread that holds them together. Can you imagine that thread existing between you and Pamela?"

She nodded her head, his casual reference to her motherless childhood clutching at her throat. "I'll try."

She spoke the line again, and Alex sat back, obviously satisfied.

The scene went on, not too badly. He had gone over blocking with her and though she knew she made some mistakes, he said nothing. By the end of the second act, she knew she had done him a great disservice thinking that he would humiliate her on the stage. He was cool, polite—all business. There was nothing in his manner to suggest that he had a relationship with her of any kind other than a professional one. When the rehearsal was over, though, and she gathered up her purse and prepared to leave, he stopped her with a hand on her arm.

"I'd like to go over the first part of act three and all of act four with you tomorrow morning at my house."

She wanted desperately to refuse him, to say she was busy or any one of a hundred other things that raced through her mind, but of course she couldn't. She lifted her head. "All right. I'll be there."

When she got into the car to go to Alex's house the next

morning, thunder rumbled in the distance. Gray clouds obscured the sun and the lake roiled angrily against the shore. The wild and untamed lake and sky somehow fit her mood. She drove to Alex's house, and by the time she parked her small car in his parking lot, the first drops of rain spattered against the windshield. She ran to his door, but as she stood under the overhang, she could feel her dampened T-shirt sticking to her skin. Then the door swung open, and Alex stood there in a dark gray silk robe. His legs and feet bare, his eyes flickering over her, he seemed more male and dangerous than ever. There was a moment when that flare of gold flamed in his eyes. Then it disappeared and a slow smile lifted the corner of his mouth. "Come in."

She hesitated, her senses screaming awareness of him. Then, as if she had no control of her legs, they moved her body into his house. As conscious of the sound of the rain on the roof as if it were drumming in her own bloodstream, she listened to the hypnotic pattern beating like the sound of distant drums, eerily relentless, more than a little alarming.

He shut the door and the dangerous sense of intimacy increased a hundredfold. His bronzed skin gleamed through the robe that was open to the tie at his waist. The clinging contours of the silk left little doubt that he wore nothing underneath. He must have come directly from the shower; his hair glistened with moisture and his body emitted a clean, woodsy fragrance.

With a show of boldness she was far from feeling, she took a step into the living room and faced the huge windows. The lovely view was gone. The rain beat against the panes of glass and a haze of gray covered sky and lake. Behind her, his footsteps moved away and then sounded on the kitchen floor. "I apologize for not being dressed. I overslept this morning. Would you like some coffee?"

She forced herself to turn and say, "Yes, please."

The sound of the rain on the roof and the sight of him robbed her of speech. Conscious of him to the tips of her toes, she climbed onto the stool.

He had already made the coffee and was pouring hers from a glass carafe. His own cup was full. He hitched his robe up and sat on the other side of the counter. "You're early for our session," he said blandly, watching her.

She took a breath and clasped her hands around the warm mug. "Yes—yes, I guess I am." She raised her eyes to his. She should be thinking about Hedvig, trying to get into character. Then why was it all she could think about was the contrast between the gray silk and his bronzed skin and how much she wanted to touch the gleaming material . . . and the hard flesh underneath?

He arched a dark eyebrow at her silence.

She took a breath. The only way to clear the air between them was to attack the problem head on. "I want to say that—that I'm sorry about the other night. I don't normally—" she swallowed, "fling myself at men. If—if I embarrassed you, I can only say that—that it won't happen again. I'd had too much wine . . ."

"But not enough to be unaware of what you were doing."

"I knew what I was doing, but—" She wanted her words to come out forcefully. Instead, they came out in a breathy husk of sound that was almost like an—invitation. "I—don't want you to think that I really meant that I—I wanted you to make love to me."

The wind blew, and the rhythm of the rain on the glass panes quickened into a fierce little rat-a-tat. He relaxed slightly against the counter and seemed to give her words careful consideration.

"In other words, you were lying."

His cool remark brought the anger back to her veins in a heated flood. "I'd had too much wine," she said again.

"But not enough to be unaware of what you were doing," he repeated bluntly. "You admit that at least. I knew you remembered every minute of it. Your face told me that the first night of rehearsal."

"All right," she said, squaring her shoulders and meeting his eyes head on with the light of battle in her own. "I made a mistake. I was intoxicated—and you were the consummate gentleman. If I caused you any—distress, I apologize. I—I'm sure by now you've forgotten the whole thing—as I have."

"Yes." The word was soft and, on the surface, agreeable. Then why did she have the feeling he was baiting her?

She lifted the cup to her lips and took a sip of coffee. It was warm and tasty and helped take the acrid taste from her mouth. She set the cup down on the table and moistened her lips. "Then we understand each other."

"Yes—you could say that." His eyes glinted with amusement, but there was a lazy sensuality about the way he was looking at her mouth that made her pulse rate soar. She was suddenly aware that her T-shirt was damp and clinging.

"And you'll stay out of my life from now on?"

He thought for a moment and then said slowly, "That's rather asking the impossible, wouldn't you say?"

"I mean my personal life."

"The statement still stands."

"Being my director doesn't mean we're personally involved—"

"We're already—involved." Each word was hard, precise, glittering like a diamond.

There was a long, tense silence. Only the sound of the rain seemed alive.

"No," she said hotly. She stared at him and made a move as if to rise. His hand snaked out, catching hers in a hard grip.

"You want me to believe that that night meant nothing to you, don't you? You want me out of your life because you can't face the fact that you let a little honest emotion show for once through that mask you call Cathy."

She stared at him. "Honest emotion—"

He met her gaze steadily. "Yes. That night—for once in your life, you were honest. You wanted me—and you said so. I applauded your forthrightness—even though I knew you were in no condition to follow through."

"I would never have—followed through." She moved slightly,

feeling a need to run out into the cleansing rain—because she was lying to him.

"Wouldn't you?" His smile mocked her. "Well, we'll never know, will we?" He rose from the stool as if he were suddenly bored with the conversation. "Excuse me for a moment, won't you? I'm going to get dressed."

His halting gait took him up the stairs. She twisted around and leaned her elbows back on the counter, a confused tangle of emotions warring in her head. She was caught—both physically and mentally. She wanted very badly to turn and walk out that door and be far, far away by the time Alex came down the stairs . . . but she couldn't. She had an obligation to the rest of the cast. She was enough of a realist to know that there was some truth in the things Alex said. She felt guilty for any number of reasons. From the very first she had mismanaged her relationships with the men in her life. If, when she was younger, she had been honest with her father and admitted her insecurities and fears, he might have reassured her—and helped her become a stronger, more realistic woman. A woman not so easily swayed by a dashing older man like Wade Warren. She might have been more prepared to stave off Wade's onslaught on her emotions and not been rushed into marriage.

The strange part of it was, she had been wary with Alex from the very first—and her wariness only seemed to draw him more deeply into her life.

The sound of his step on the stairs intruded on her thoughts and he came into view, disturbingly all together in black denim pants molded to his lean hips, and a burgundy shirt open half-way down his chest.

He gestured toward the bare space in front of the windows. "We'll let that be your backdrop. Visualize the passageway to your right." He arranged furniture deftly, while she was left struggling to match his businesslike demeanor.

He took her through act three slowly, blocking as they went. It was the most difficult of all, for several reasons. In the first scene, her speeches were interspersed at random intervals with the others so that there was the problem of what to do, how to stand and where to look while the other actors were saying their lines. Then, in the last climactic moment of her appearance, she must act out in pantomime her fright and horror at being rejected by her father and snatch the pistol from the shelf, ostensibly to kill the wild duck Gregers has asked her to sacrifice—but in reality, to kill herself.

Alex did not like the way she performed the final scene. She did it over and over, and when she had finished for the sixth time, he said slowly, "No. It's better—but it's still not right, I don't know exactly why. Do it again."

Something inside her head exploded. She whirled away and stood looking out into the gray day. "I knew I wouldn't be able to please you—"

He grasped her shoulders and pulled her back against him. "Damn you, woman, that's what's wrong. You're focusing on me instead of the role." He turned her around to face him. "You have it in you to be Hedvig, Cathy. You know what it is to want and need a father's love—and be denied it."

"Oh, God, no." She buried her face against the smooth fabric of his shirt, fighting to maintain her sanity while inside her the barricade broke and all the flood waters of emotion burst through. "Years," she sobbed. "Years and years—wasted . . ." She lifted her head. She couldn't let Alex think her father was to blame. "I've been hating him for years . . . and it wasn't his fault. . . ."

She couldn't stop crying. She sobbed against his shirt and he held her in the warm circle of his arms and said nothing. When her sobbing abated, he said, "Cathy." The word was husky and possessive. "Tell me."

She shook her head silently, and his grip tightened. "You can tell me."

She did then, in a low, halting voice, spilling it all out in a jumbled chaos of emotion, how she had shut her father out—and believed that he was shutting her out. When she finished, she looked up into his eyes, hoping she might see a flicker of understanding and affection. Instead, she saw . . . compassion.

Anguish filled her. *He feels sorry for you. He's going to kiss you because he pities you. . . .*

She wrenched away, ran to the door, and tugged at it viciously. It flew open and she propelled herself out into the rain.

"Cathy! Get back in here . . ." His voice was sharp, commanding, but she ignored it and ran in the direction of her car. The rain was not falling heavily, but the wind blew fat drops off the leaves of the trees into her face. She reached her car, only to realize that she had no key and that Alex was coming out of the house at a dead run. She whirled and ran, scrambling up the hill to the road. At the edge, she paused for a second, considering. If she ran down the highway, Alex would see her and catch her in a minute, despite his halting gait. On the other side, another hill barred her way. It was covered with dense, scrubby brush. She made her decision and raced across the road to lunge at the steep incline of wet earth, digging her sneakers into the slippery grass, sliding, falling back, scratching her face on the brush, catching her sleeve on the thorn of a wild raspberry bush. With a cry of fury, she tore free and plunged on. If she got to the top of the hill before Alex saw her, she could hide in the undergrowth. She panted and climbed, driven upward by the sheer force of her anxiety and fear. Footsteps crashed in the brush behind her and she increased her efforts, tugging frantically at little bushes to help her maintain her fight against the pull of gravity as she climbed higher. Then she was at the top and over, running through the tall trees on the other side down into a tiny valley where a stream ran heavy with the new-fallen rain.

Under the cover of a sprawling bush she hesitated, uncertain which way to go. When she heard footsteps pounding the earth behind her, she tensed her muscles and whirled to run—only to feel Alex's hard hand on her shoulder. She twisted and wildly attempted to pull away.

"For God's sake! Stop it, Cathy!"

Her sneakers slipped on the wet earth. She tottered, fighting to stay on her feet and wrench free of that hard grip, but she lost the battle and fell backward into the rain-wet earth, dragging him with her. He lay sprawled across her, his dazed face telling her that the fall had stunned him momentarily. She arched her body to heave him upward and free herself before he could regain his senses. It was too late. He came to life; hard hands shackled her wrists and her arms were crossed and pressed over her head with his hard weight baring down on her. He leaned over her and stared down into her face. She tossed her head ineffectually. He growled out a savage word and let the full weight of his body pin her chest to the ground.

"Cathy." His face loomed over her. Water dripped from the strands of his black hair and fell on her cheek. His burgundy shirt was mottled with moisture.

"Let me go, Alex."

His breathing was fast and rasping. "Why?"

She stared at him, her violet eyes cold, her breasts heaving under his arms. "I don't want your pity."

His lips twisted, his voice low and savagely harsh. "What I'm feeling right now isn't pity."

She met his eyes, her courage burning in the bright violet pupils. "But it isn't love."

The rain streamed down into her face and made her dark lashes spiky. The smell of damp grass and crushed wild roses surrounded her.

"What do you think it is?"

His words were harsh and insistent and she didn't want to answer them, but his arms on her chest nudged her to speech. "Desire, lust, I don't know. Why do you insist on labeling it?"

He said hoarsely, "Because that's the way you like things, all neatly labeled. This much love for your father, that much love received from him. All wrapped up and neatly labeled. Why don't you grow up and face the truth—that love exists even when it's not expressed or acknowledged?" He stopped for a moment, his eyes locked on hers. "And do you know what frightens you most of all?" He paused to give his words effect and she waited, the gleam in his eyes stealing her breath. The hard pounding of her heart must have been evident to him through his knuckles that were welded to her chest. "You're afraid your love for me is going to be as hopeless as your love for your father or for Wade."

Writhing under his hands, she cried, "No . . ."

"Yes." His eyes impaled her. She twisted her head to avoid them.

Impatiently, he gripped her hands tighter and shook them. "Admit the truth, damn you!"

She turned back, her temper warming every cell in her body. "Why should I? You care nothing for me!"

The silence stretched. She held her breath, and the rain fell in her face and she knew she had thrown the angry challenge at him, hoping against all reason that he'd deny it.

His words were strangely distant. "If I said I did—would you believe me?"

Hope blazed up in her . . . until she looked into his face. There was not a flicker of interest in her answer. He might have been talking to a stone. But she wasn't a stone. Every feminine nerve was registering the hard pressure of his thighs against hers. "No, I wouldn't believe you. Now, let me up."

He shook his head slowly.

"Alex . . ."

"No," he murmured, bending his head.

If he kissed her, she would be lost. "Don't," she muttered, twisting her head. "I don't want your pity," she insisted.

He tensed with anger. "Then you damn well won't get it." With her hands flattened to the ground on each side of her head, she lay pinned in front of him like a prisoner, exposed, and helpless to stop his eyes from traveling over the lift of her cheekbone, down to the intimate hollows of her throat, and lower, over the wet, rounded curves of her breasts.

His eyes heated her skin as his hands had that day in his bedroom. Her heart thudded till she thought he must see its movement against the wet shirt. The slow, languorous throbbing of desire began deep in her loins. She met his eyes steadily.

"And with it all," he murmured, "you have courage—"

He bent his head. His mouth was warm against the coolness of hers, masculine and firm and totally persuasive. He held her captive not by force, but by the blaze of emotion that welled up inside her. A longing to hold him made her move her hands restlessly under his grip. As if he understood, he freed them at once. She moved her arms to clasp them around his neck and draw him closer. Her senses were filled with him, the wet fabric of his shirt under her palms, the provocative musky male smell of his body, the feel of his tongue erotically exploring her mouth. He was elemental and real, a part of the earth and the rain—and she needed him desperately.

He pulled his mouth from hers and she moaned a soft protest. He looked at her long and thoughtfully. Then he smiled, and it was as if the sun had suddenly appeared. "You've got mud on your nose."

Why was it Alex could switch moods . . . and take her with him so skillfully? "Thanks a lot." Her voice held a dry amusement. "You're very romantic."

He leaned closer, a wicked gleam of amusement in his eyes. "Actually," he said softly, "I was thinking of how much I'm going to enjoy washing you off."

"Alex, I . . ." Restlessly, she turned her head to avoid his eyes.

He caught her chin in his hard fingers and brought it sharply back, forcing her to look at him. "Don't play games with me, Cathy. Games are for children." He let his eyes drop to her mouth and then wander slowly over the soaked T-shirt. "And you're long past childhood."

He eased his weight away, got to his feet and held out his hand. "Come back to the house with me."

Oblivious to the rain, she stared up at him and knew that if she put her hand in his, there would be no turning back. She knew equally well that if she refused his hand, he would turn and walk away without a backward glance.

She extended her arm. He caught her cold fingers in his warm ones and pulled her to her feet. "Come on," he said, his voice filled with laughter. "We look like we've been rehearsing for the heath scene from *King Lear*!"

Holding hands, they charged at the hill, laughing, scrambling, their feet sliding on the slippery grass. The sound of his warm, deep laughter was sheer delight to her ears. She could take on the world as long as Alex was at her side, laughing like that. They crested the hill and half-ran, half-tumbled through the brush down to the bottom. At the road, they were forced to stand dripping on the side, waiting for a car to pass. The driver, a man, gaped at them. Alex gave him a cheery wave and Cathy laughed at the man's startled expression. When the car had moved safely ahead of them, Alex tightened his grip and pulled her across the road.

They were still laughing when they reached the house. "Maybe he thinks I'm Gene Kelly."

"Not a chance," she shot back. "You don't have the umbrella."

"But I have you," he murmured. Outside the door, with the drops of rain still falling around them, he pulled her close to give her a hard kiss. It was a frankly intimate one that claimed her as his woman.

The wind whipped against them, and he broke away reluctantly. She struggled for self-control, feeling his hand at her back as he pushed her into the house. He let his hand slide sensuously down her thigh before he stooped to pull off her shoes. His hands on her ankles were another sweet promise of things to come—and destroyed what little remaining poise she had left. He didn't seem to notice her distracted state and he straightened and smiled at her. "You're a pretty sight, I'll say that," brushing the end of her nose with his finger. "Mud from end to end." His hand cupped around her rear and he gave her a gentle push. "Up you get and into the shower."

She didn't need a second invitation. She ran up the stairs, her feet making damp foot outlines on the wooden treads. She shut herself in the bathroom, stripped out of her clothes and stepped into the shower. In the roomy cubicle, Alex had installed a shelf, and she adjusted the water to a steamy hot and reached for the shampoo.

She had just finished rinsing her dark hair when she heard the sound she had been unconsciously waiting for. The shower door opened, and Alex stepped in, naked and gorgeously male. Her stomach plummeted. He shut the door behind him and stood very still for a moment, his eyes traveling slowly down her slim, wet body. Then he said huskily, "Hand me the soap."

Unable to do anything else, she retrieved it from the shelf and placed it in his hands.

He began at her shoulders, moving his soap-slicked hands in slow circles over the rounded bones. His fingers slid down a path to the valley between her breasts. She felt a heavy warmth beating in her veins, and an almost intolerable suspense as she waited for him to discover the rosy peaks that were taut with anticipation. When at last he cupped her breasts, she shuddered with pleasure. He let his hands slide lower to her navel, her abdomen, and her thighs. Then he bent and gave his special loving attention to her ankles and toes. When she thought sensual pleasure would overwhelm her, he rose and pulled her into his arms. His soapy hands went around her to lather her back and hips. Tingling sensations of need began deep within and radiated through her. The hard leanness of his water-slick body was imprinted on her. He was playing the part of her personal servant, performing that most intimate of tasks, but she was the one who was enslaved by his caressive hands.

He released her from his embrace and said, "Here. Take the soap."

He rinsed his hands and then cupped them, gently redirecting the spray of water, bombarding her body to rinse away the suds. She rotated slowly and when she faced him again, his cupped hands tossed water at her breasts and shoulders, drenching her in sensual pleasure.

Then it was her turn. She reveled in the freedom to massage

his body with her soapy hands, loving the feel of the hair-crisp skin of his chest against her palms. His back was satiny and smooth, with hard muscle and bone underneath. Her hands wandered over him and down, tracing the path of the cruel scar on his thigh.

When she had rinsed him with splashes of water, she raised her face to him. He stood as if he were letting his eyes feast on the sight of her. Then with a soft groan, he pulled her into his arms and kissed her. She was on fire with sensation, the water running warm and silky over her skin, his hands sliding possessively over her wet hips and back, his tongue probing her mouth.

With dreamlike slowness, he released her and turned off the flow of water. He drew her with him out of the cubicle and slowly, with a fluffy bath towel and infinite gentleness, he dried her. When she had done the same for him, he lifted her naked body into his arms and carried her out of the bathroom. "I seem to remember doing this once before." His eyes flashed down at her, taking in the creamy length of her lying in his arms.

A teasing smile lifted her lips. "At least I had a towel on then."

"I like you much better this way, my love." He lowered her from the cradle of his arms to the bed and followed her down to stretch out beside her.

My love. He said the two words casually, and they meant nothing to him, but they sent such a depth charge of feeling through her, she propped herself on one elbow and trailed a questing fingernail through the dark hair on his chest. "And I like you much better this way . . . my love."

Her words seemed to have no visible effect on him. He draped a casual hand around her neck and pulled her to him. "Kiss me," he muttered, his warm breath caressing her mouth.

An impish urge to tease him made her lower her mouth very slowly to his and then, with the lightness of a butterfly's wing, touch the top of his lip with hers. She explored the contours of his mouth slowly, nibbling gently at the upper curve, her tongue deftly touching his fuller, lower one.

He tolerated her exquisite torture until she thought he must be immune to her light toying with his lips. Then a shudder racked his body, and he twisted upward violently and rolled to trap her under him.

Slowly, huskily, with a thread of laughter in his throat, he said, "For that, you'll pay, woman . . . and pay dearly."

"I already have," she breathed, thinking she had fallen so deeply in love with him, she would never be free again.

"No," he contradicted in a seductive murmur, moving his hands to the sensitive skin of her throat, "you haven't even begun."

He eased his weight away and with tender and loving attention, he traced around the circumference of her breasts. Her taut peaks quivered for his touch, but he carefully avoided them and let his hand wander down the valley of her breasts to her navel and back up again around the side of her to the delicate base of her throat.

"Alex . . ."

"What is it, my love?" his tone light, mocking.

"Alex, please—touch me—"

"But I am touching you." His hand trailed down the silken length of her thigh.

A moan escaped her throat. "Alex, I—"

"Patience, my love, patience." He bent to her and where his hands had caressed, his lips set her on fire with want and need. She raked his shoulders with her fingernails, her body in a frenzied state of waiting.

A low sound like the satisfied purr of a tiger came from his throat. His lips took a leisurely path back to her breasts and then he moved, covering her nipple with his mouth.

She gasped and clung to him. He lifted his head and eased her torment—only to take her other breast in his mouth and tease its taut crest to an aching peak with his tongue.

Her body arched involuntarily. "Alex, please, please, no more . . ."

He laughed softly. "Do you imagine I'd let you off that easily? Ah, you don't know me very well yet, do you, darling?" He lifted his head and his hands discovered her all over again, lingering in the secret feminine places of her, bringing a devastating delight. He was taking her to heaven and beyond. She longed to tell him how much she loved him, but instead she whispered his name in an aching sound of longing. His erotic pleasuring lengthened into tortured rapture—until at last, he heeded her whispered pleadings and made her his.

If she thought she had seen heaven before, she knew she had only glimpsed a far horizon. With him, for the first time in her life, she was complete, whole. When she had experienced as much pleasure as she had ever known, he took her on a new, soaring flight that peaked in an explosion of passion into ecstasy.

When it was over, he held her gently, letting her float slowly to earth with him again.

A moment later, he lifted his weight and rolled to one side, but a possessive hand returned to cup her breast. He leaned on an elbow and looked down at her with a dark, unreadable expression. She tried to guess at his thoughts, but she couldn't.

"What do you see?" she asked, wanting desperately to know what was going on behind that lean, enigmatic face.

"I see a woman who has been quite thoroughly made love to," was his amused reply.

She had hoped for something more, she wasn't just sure what. When she frowned, he leaned forward and brushed her forehead with his lips. He trailed kisses over her eyes, her nose, her mouth. "What do you see, my love?" There was a quiet, waiting quality in his words.

She lay in the languid aftermath of his lovemaking, wanting more than anything to confess all the love that was in her heart. Silently, she studied the way his dark hair grew back from his forehead and then lifted a hand and touched the silken strands.

"I see the man who made love to her." But doesn't love her, her mind mocked, and her hand fell back to the bed, away from him.

Her answer seemed to dissatisfy him. Something came and went in his face. Then he asked casually, "Tired?"

"A little." She forced her voice to sound light and teasing. "I did run up a hill, you know."

"And down again," he said huskily, giving her a quick, hard kiss. "Close your eyes now and rest." He drew the brown silken sheet up over her. "You have time for a nap before rehearsal."

Her eyes flew wide open. "Rehearsal! I'd forgotten all about rehearsal."

"I rather thought you had." His smile was sleek and self-satisfied.

But he hadn't, her mind whispered.

She raised herself up. "I'd better go . . ."

He pushed her back into the pillow with hard hands on her shoulders. "No," he said coolly. "You're not going anywhere."

She struggled to escape him. "But I have to go home and get fresh clothes and—"

"You can do that later," he said, a hint of iron under the soft tones. "Right now, you're going to stay in my bed. Here, with me. And if you don't sleep," his eyes flickered down over the outline of her that was plainly visible under the silken sheet, "I'll find something else for you to do." He lowered his head. "Perhaps I will, anyway."

"No—Alex—"

"Yes, Cathy," he said, covering his mouth with hers, pulling the sheet away to let his palm discover the warm feminine contours of her all over again.

CHAPTER TEN

A mirror ran the width of the backstage dressing room. Cathy leaned forward and applied deep violet eyeshadow to the lids of her eyes with cold and shaky hands. It was a moment she had waited for all her life, the moment she had feared would never come. It was opening night of *The Wild Duck,* and she should have been wild with excitement. Instead, she was depressed and disturbed.

True, Alex and she had both been busy. True, rehearsals had been long and exhausting. True, she needed to focus every bit of her energy on absorbing the role of Hedvig into her own personality.

But his determined, impersonal coolness during rehearsals had nearly destroyed her. It was only because she had learned long ago how to immerse her own emotions in those she was creating on the stage, that she had survived.

She needed him. Like an ache inside her, she needed his arms around her, needed his kiss on her lips, needed the feel of his body pressing against hers. How long would this lack of any real communication between them go on? Had Alex merely been intrigued by her coolness, and now that the chase was over—lost interest?

A cold knot tightened in her stomach. She couldn't believe that. He had cared enough for her to want to help her untangle the raveled skein of her relationship with her father. Surely there was more for them. Surely he cared to make something of the turbulent relationship . . .

Nervously, she peered in the mirror. Was her makeup right? She had used a much lighter shade of eyeliner and mascara to create the illusion of youth that Alex wanted and dramatically heightened the depth of her violet eyes with shadow. She snapped the cap back on the tube of her base makeup and tossed it in her case. She left her makeup cape on; Millie had not yet styled her hair. She was with Pamela, arranging her blond tresses lovingly.

Cathy thrust her hands in her lap to stop them from trembling. *You're a fine professional actress. You've committed the cardinal sin of falling in love with the director—and now you've got a bad double dose of opening night nerves—because you're afraid you'll fail the man you love!*

Why wouldn't she be frightened? There were people coming from all over the country to see if Alex had retained his genius touch with Ibsen. *Cactus Flower* had been a success, true, but the real test of Alex's directing skill would be judged by the more serious and difficult Ibsen play. Friends of Alex's had flown in from California that morning. She hadn't heard if anyone from New York City had arrived. Perhaps they would come later, after the play had run a week. And that would be another test . . .

Oh, God, somehow, she had to stop thinking of Alex. She had to concentrate on getting into character—now. A moment's slip of concentration out there on the stage and the illusion was destroyed.

She lifted her head and stared at her mirrored reflection. Out of the corner of her eye, she saw Pamela studying her with a thoughtful expression.

"I get all the movie magazines," Millie announced, her hands moving quickly over Pamela's hair, tucking the silver star away under a curl where it wouldn't be seen. Alex had forbidden even a glimpse of it. Gina was not a woman to wear silver stars. "I think I saw your picture in one once. Did I?"

Pamela shrugged. "You might have. I've given several interviews in the last few years."

"I read an article about Mr. Reardon. It was all about him, about what a swell director he was, and how his leading ladies all fall in love with him." Millie had everyone's interest now, even the quiet Anne Grant, the woman who was playing the part of Mrs. Sorby.

Pamela's finely drawn brows flew up. "You know, Millie, not everything you read in print is true."

Millie, whose red hair tumbled about her head in unruly curls that looked as if they had never seen a comb, glanced up at Pamela's reflection with a shocked look on her face. "Oh, I'm sure they wouldn't dare print anything that wasn't the truth. I mean, there are laws against things like that—aren't there, Ms. Taylor?"

"Yes, of course," Cathy murmured, knowing that Millie deferred to her for the last word on law because of her father's profession.

"Anyway," Millie went on chattily, undeterred, "this article told all about his directing techniques and how he uses some guy's theories, that Russian with the crazy-sounding name—"

"Stanislavski," Pamela supplied with a dry impatience.

"Yes, that was it." Excited now and building up steam, Millie careened on. "But the part of the article I loved was where it told how he believes in getting personally involved with the members of his cast. Especially his leading ladies." Millie's voice dropped to a low, confidential tone. "The article quoted him as saying he believes making love frees the emotions and puts people in touch with themselves. I thought that was so beautiful."

A forgotten echo of words exploded inside her head. *Watch out for Reardon. He doesn't hesitate to make love to a woman if he thinks she will work harder because she believes he's in love with her.*

The blood drained away from her face. In the bright light she looked completely colorless, almost ghostly.

"Maybe that depends on your point of view," Pamela said sharply.

"But I know it's true what that magazine said. Why, everyone knows he's madly in love with you—" Millie stammered to a stop at the fiery look Pamela sent her in the mirror.

"Just finish up with my hair, Millie. Please."

Pamela's eyes met Cathy's in the mirror. The silence went on and on, until at last a chastened Millie fixed Cathy's hair into the two bunches on each side of her head that Alex wanted, gathered up her brushes and combs, and left.

"Anne, if you're ready, could you possibly go and see if Larry found that other sewing basket I wanted? I've got to re-do my makeup a bit."

"Yes, of course."

When the door closed, Pamela turned to a silent, frozen Cathy.

"Don't let anything that woman said throw you. You know what garbage they print occasionally just to fill space."

She tried for a cool, "I don't know what you're talking about . . ." but Pamela was not fooled.

"Yes, you do," Pamela said implacably. "you've gone white as a ghost. You are in love with Alex, aren't you?"

She knew there was little use in denying it but she couldn't admit the truth. A quick, negative shake of her head did not deter Pamela, who replied crisply, "Let me give you a small piece of advice from someone who knows." Her eyes met Cathy's in the mirror and Cathy braced herself.

"Don't listen to anything anyone says—and don't let him go. If he's half as interested in you as I think he is, you're a lucky woman."

Cathy sat, stunned. Pamela rose, but continued fussing with her hair.

"Why are you telling me this?" Cathy whispered.

Pamela's smile was slightly twisted, mocking. "Self-preservation," she said simply. "If you go out on that stage as emotionally blitzed as you were a moment ago, you're going to bomb. And you'll take me right along with you." She paused and gazed at Cathy. "I don't want that to happen."

"No," Cathy was torn between laughter and tears, "I don't

suppose you do." Pamela had all but professed to love Alex—yet she had not mentioned a word about the damage to his career if Cathy failed. She thought only of her own.

"So," Pamela said, with the air of a doctor who has just given the patient good news, "let's cheer up. We both have a marvelous chance to further our careers tonight. Let's not muff it, shall we?" She walked to the mirror and picked up the kerchief that was a part of her costume. She wrapped it around her head with a few expert twists and looked into the mirror again. "Ugh. This thing is horrible. But I suppose if I must, I must." With a return to her characteristic preoccupation with herself, she said critically, "At least my dress has a little more color in it than yours. If Alex had told me to wear that brown thing, I think I'd have thrown it in his face."

She gazed at Cathy. "Are you sure that dress won't affect your acting?"

It was a release of tension to laugh. "No," she assured Pamela, "the dress won't affect my acting."

Waiting through the first act was the worst. By the time the curtain fell, her palms were clammy with perspiration and her heart was pounding in her chest. She clung to the side curtain, her stomach in turmoil, an almost physical sickness welling up in her throat. To make matters worse, Alex strolled backstage, looking lean and disturbingly masculine in a summer suit of light gray that she had never seen before.

"Darling, you look gorgeous," Pamela said from somewhere behind her.

"Thank you," he replied with a mocking smile, but his eyes were on Cathy. "How are you holding up?"

She only nodded, hating him a little because he looked cool and completely in control.

"Did the first act go well?" Pamela asked.

"One little fluff, but otherwise okay."

"What kind of audience is it?"

"Quiet, attentive."

"John and Nina are pleased?"

A quick frown furrowed his brow. "Yes, so far."

"And Farrin, has he said anything?"

Alex shot her a dark look. "You know Farrin never says anything until he sits down to write his column."

Cathy asked, "Who is Farrin?"

"A critic for the *San Francisco Examiner,*" Pamela said complacently.

Cathy had difficulty finding her voice. "And he's reviewing this play?"

Alex reached out and caught her hand, his open suit jacket moving over his lean hips. "He's a personal friend. He may give the play something of a mention in his Sunday column, a quick comment or two, nothing to worry about."

"What a lot of lovely friends you have, Alex," Pamela mocked.

A sardonic look flashed Pamela's way. "I'd better go. Here's a kiss for luck." He pulled Cathy close and touched the tip of her nose with his mouth. "Relax, darling. You'll be wonderful."

"What about me?" Pamela asked.

Alex turned reluctantly away from Cathy and leaned over to touch his lips lightly to Pamela's cheek. "You're an old hand at being wonderful," he said cryptically and strolled off the stage, unaware of the hot look Pamela sent him.

"Places. Take your places, please."

Both she and Pamela hurried to follow the stage manager's directions.

She had always thought stage acting was something like going for a ride on a roller coaster. There was the sickness and anticipation beforehand, but once you began, you were swept along on an irretrievable course. There was nothing to do but continue. If you had done your work well, and were lucky, you got caught up in the story and forgot everything except the character you were creating.

She knew the play was going well. The second act progressed to the third and fourth. The cast outdid themselves, going from strength to strength until the climactic end. When Cathy pulled the gun from the shelf, she heard a gasp from the audience and knew that she had indeed succeeded in conveying to them the tragedy of what she was about to do.

The final curtain fell, and they took several bows to enthusiastic applause. When the curtain call was over, she felt a mixture of emotions—relief, disappointment, an anxiety to know if other people thought it was as good as it felt to her. She was on that old familiar emotional high and she knew she wouldn't come down for hours.

Backstage, Alex stood in a circle of people whom Cathy did not recognize. They were the friends Pamela had mentioned, she supposed. A man who, with his iron gray hair and high forehead, looked more like a judge than her father stood talking to Alex. A handsome woman with dark hair and a graceful way of holding her head stood on the other side. Pamela was there, too, her hand tucked possessively under Alex's arm, her face beaming radiantly up at him.

They were the charmed circle, the people who had already achieved success. After tonight, Alex belonged to that group again.

Cathy went into the dressing room, her emotional high plunging to depression. She had not wanted to believe the truth of Millie's words—and Ellen's—but Alex had not once looked her way or signaled her over. Perhaps they had both been right. Perhaps her usefulness to Alex was ended. Was he that cold and callous? She didn't think so. But what did she know of him, really? Did she know the man under that professional veneer?

She had shared a bed with him, but little else. He was a consummate actor, she knew that. She knew he didn't love her. Had even his passion been an act? Deeply disturbed, she undressed and began to cream off her makeup. The door opened and Pamela entered the room. "Cathy! We've been looking all over for you. Alex wants to introduce you to George Farrin and his wife."

She arranged her face in a cool expression and made a deprecatory gesture over her slim body clad in pants and bra. "I'm hardly dressed to meet people."

"Well, get dressed," Pamela ordered her impatiently, "and come along to Alex's house later." She snatched up her makeup kit. "I'm going to do my face and change there."

She thought of Pamela in Alex's bedroom and did not drive to the house. She went instead to her father's house. It was dark when she arrived, but after she opened the door and walked in, she saw the light streaming into the hallway from her father's study. The clock chimed the half-hour. The sound of the ticking accompanied her as she started to climb the stairs. Midway, her father's voice halted her.

"Cathy?"

She lay a hand on the smooth bannister. "Yes?"

Jason Taylor came out of his study. He stood looking up at her from the hallway. The light shone on his hair and it was ruffled, as if he had run his hand through it several times that evening. It was the first time she had seen him looking less than composed.

"You didn't go to Alex's?"

"No, I—" She faltered and then said, "I decided to come home and get some rest."

He peered up at her, his eyes traveling over her white, still face. "You look as if you need it." She stood silently, submitting to his perusal. "Is something wrong?"

She lifted her chin slightly. "What could possibly be wrong, Father?"

He frowned, as if she had asked him a complicated legal question he had to consider carefully. "Will you come out in the kitchen and have some coffee with me? I'd like to talk to you for a moment."

She hesitated, a polite refusal on the tip of her tongue. She was shaken by her thoughts about Alex and the last thing in the world that she wanted at this moment was polite conversation with her father, but if he was trying to open a line of communication, she felt compelled to make an effort to meet him halfway.

"All right," she said and turned around on the stair.

She knew her emotional stress had to be there on her face for him to read in the bright lights of the kitchen.

He pulled two yellow mugs from the shelf and poured coffee into them. "Do you use anything—"

"Nothing, Father, just black."

He splashed his own drink with milk and sat down across from her on the high stool at the butcher block table. He was quiet for a moment. Then he said, "I wanted to thank you for your kindness to Audrey."

She traced a finger around the handle of the cup. She didn't know what she had expected, but it wasn't this. "It's not difficult to be kind to her, father." She met his hazel eyes candidly.

"I have to admit I was—concerned. Cam had already met her—but you—you hadn't, and I was apprehensive . . ."

"I'm not a little girl anymore, Father. I do realize you have a right to live your own life and I'm pleased you've found someone to love who—loves you."

Her father looked down at his cup. "You were—outstanding in the play tonight, Catherine. I was—very proud of you—and a little envious, I think."

He threw her a quick, challenging look and she was jarred. She sensed that that admission did not come easily to him.

She smiled faintly. "Do you nourish a hidden ambition to be on the stage, Father?"

"Of course." A slight smile lifted his lips. "Don't all lawyers? Where did you think you got your talent? Your mother was an extremely shy woman."

"Was she? I never knew that. In her pictures, she was always smiling."

"Yes," he said thoughtfully, his eyes gazing at something over her shoulder. "She was the joy in my life. When she died, she took that joy with her." He focused his gaze on her. "Seeing you in that play—taught me something." Another long pause. Then his shoulders heaved slightly. "I've done you a great disservice, Catherine."

Tears welled in her eyes. She dropped long lashes over them. "Don't blame yourself, father."

"We've never understood each other very well, have we? We lost her, and we were both angry. Instead of loving you more, I shut you out of my life because it hurt so much just to look at you." He pressed his lips together as if he were still remembering the pain. "When you were older, I tried to talk to you but you reacted like a spitting young wildcat fighting for survival." The fine lines around his mouth deepened. "I suppose you were, really. You had been deprived of love. Now, all that longing pours out of you on the stage. You make the audience long to love you and make up for what you've lost."

"Then something good has come of my life, hasn't it?" she said easily. "I bring pleasure to other people."

"Yes, pleasure to others. But what about yourself? Melissa tells me you haven't been too happy these last two weeks . . ."

The old protective barrier made her smile faintly and murmur, "No, not happy. But surviving, father. Surviving."

Her answer didn't please him. "Is that your goal, then? To survive?"

"Right at the moment—yes."

"Cathy—about Alex—"

She braced herself—and as if it were a cue in a play, the ring of the telephone interrupted him.

He made an impatient gesture and rose to answer. "Good lord. Audrey's trying to get some rest . . ." Cathy heard him mumbling as he stepped to the phone and lifted the receiver from the wall.

After a brusque greeting, his voice took on a warmer tone. "Yes, she's here." He put his hand over the mouthpiece. "Cathy. It's Alex."

Reluctantly, she got off the stool and took the receiver her father held out to her. "Hello?"

His voice exploded into her ear. "Where the hell are you?

Didn't Pamela tell you I wanted you over here to meet Farrin and the others?"

She let her voice drop into a husky imitation of weariness. "Yes, she did. I just didn't feel up to it, Alex."

A small silence greeted her words. "You're all right, aren't you?" He didn't hide the tinge of concern in his voice but Cathy knew it was strictly professional. After all, she was important to him now—as an actress.

"I'm fine," she answered, "just a little tired."

There was another silence and then he said, "Well, get some rest. I'll see you tomorrow."

CHAPTER ELEVEN

The play ran for another two weeks, and she wasn't sure how she got through them. She couldn't sleep, couldn't eat. Somehow, she managed to go through the motions of living by establishing a routine. She lay in bed till her thoughts were no longer tolerable, got up to pick at the food Melissa prepared so lovingly, drove to the theater, steeled herself for Alex's pre-performance speech, and then melted back into the dressing room to put on makeup and get into her costume.

By some miracle, her acting wasn't affected by her state of mind. She was profoundly grateful for that. After the play, she talked to people and forgot what she said, removed her makeup and got into her car to drive home . . . alone. Alex had not addressed one word to her individually since the phone call at her father's house. At the theater he looked through her as if she didn't exist. Even though he had been that way for days, she couldn't seem to adjust to the agony of knowing he didn't really care for her. After each performance, she was numb and listless with pain. There was a party at the Willow Inn after the first week's performances of *The Wild Duck* and she had begged off, knowing it would be more than she could bear to spend several hours in proximity to Alex.

Then it was the final night of *The Wild Duck*, the last time she would act under Alex's direction.

Alex's pre-performance speech was short and complimentary.

When it was over and most of the cast had disappeared, he caught her arm. "Cathy—"

Pamela materialized beside him. "Alex, darling, is Max going to be here tonight?"

He turned a dark, hard face to her. "Yes, he's here."

A sting of fear grabbed at her throat. "Who is—Max?"

"Darling, I'm sorry." Pamela didn't sound regretful. "You haven't told her."

"No." his eyes flickered over Cathy's face.

"Who is—Max?" she asked.

"A producer," Alex said noncommittally.

"Oh, he's much more than that. He's a lovely man—with a lot of lovely money."

Alex cast a sardonic look over Pamela's smiling face. To Cathy, he said, "I'll be waiting for you after the performance. I want you to talk to him."

"Setting something up for her?" Pamela said, in a cool tone that didn't hide her envy.

"Possibly," was Alex's impatient reply. "I've got to go now." To Cathy, he said, "I'll see you afterwards."

When he left them, Pamela turned to her, and with a frosty glaze on her face, said, "Well, you will have to be extra good tonight, won't you?" and walked away.

So much for camaraderie, Cathy thought ruefully.

Despite Pamela's hostility, she found that her acting had taken on depth and meaning over the two weeks. She was beginning to know Hedvig well. Strangely enough, she would miss creating her character when the play was over.

After the final curtain call, she took off her makeup and changed her clothes with a distinct sense of regret—and relief. Now she had one more ordeal left, seeing the Max that Alex was so anxious for her to see. When she came out of the dressing room, Alex didn't seem to be about anywhere, so she went out into the warm night. In the parking lot, a man straightened away from her car, and her heart lept to her throat—until she recognized James.

"I haven't had a chance to talk to you," he said softly. His hair blew in the light summer breeze. "I wanted to tell you how much I enjoyed the play tonight."

She fastened her gaze on his white shirt open at the throat. He wore no tie and no jacket. "Thank you, James." She paused and then asked, "How is your wife—Anne?"

"She's found a small part in a play that's opening for the fall season off-Broadway. She's very excited."

"I'm glad for her," Cathy said, thrusting back a lock of dark hair.

"We've decided to stay together, if you can call it that." There was a wry twist to his mouth. "We're going to commute on weekends. She'll come to Naples when she's not working—and I'll go to New York every weekend I can get away. I have more freedom than she does—so I suppose I'll do most of the traveling." He paused and smiled. "It isn't an ideal situation—but I suppose we aren't the first couple to find our marriage doesn't fit the standard mold."

"No, I don't suppose you are, James," she agreed, thinking that she would fly to the ends of the earth every Friday night if it meant stepping into Alex's arms at the end of the trip, "But if you love each other . . ."

"Yes," he said softly. "We do—too much to end our marriage."

On an impulse, she leaned forward and touched her lips to his cheek. "A kiss for luck, James."

When she would have moved away, he pulled her close and kissed her full on the lips. "And luck to you, Cathy."

He stood staring down at her. She felt suddenly self-conscious. "Good-bye, James."

"Cathy." Alex's crisp voice cut the night air. "I've been looking for you."

"I was just talking to James—"

"I see." The night air seemed to give Alex's voice a dry, saturnine quality.

"Hello, Alex," James said easily. "I was just telling Cathy how much I enjoyed the play."

Alex had come to stand between James and Cathy, and while James was a larger man, his girth made him look vulnerable. Alex was lean and hard and there was a subtle dangerous quality about him that every nerve end in her body seemed to be reading. Another movement toward her made her pulses beat heavily. His hand on her arm only compounded her disturbance.

"Are you ready? Max doesn't like to be kept waiting."

"I'll say good night then." James nodded his head at Cathy and went to his car.

Alex gripped her arm. "Come on," he said roughly. He opened the door with his customary courtesy, but when the edge of her yellow chiffon dress fell over the doorframe, he tucked it inside and shut the door with extra vehemence.

He was angry, just why she wasn't sure. She had done what he wanted her to do. She was a success. But her success had brought failure, heart failure, she thought with a wry humor. She had fallen in love with him, desperately, deeply. But he did not love her. Like tonight, his only thought was for her career—and his own.

She thought back over the day she had spent at his house. He had worked those scenes over and over with her . . . and when her emotional turmoil threatened to ruin his efforts, he had taken her to bed.

Such dedication to art, her mind mocked sardonically, as Alex started the car and drove out of the parking lot onto the moonlit road. *He should get an award.* The cool answer came back from her mind. *But his technique worked, didn't it? Just as he had known it would!*

Alex's head turned and he looked at her for so long, she began to fear for their safety on the road. Did her appearance have some effect on him? The yellow chiffon was high-necked and long-sleeved . . . but transparent. A matching yellow satin slip with spaghetti straps kept her from indecency. She had done her hair with the curling iron, creating a romantic look to go with the dress. A light eyeshadow accented the violet color of her dark eyes.

When at last he returned his gaze to the road, he said softly, "You pulled out all the stops tonight, didn't you?"

"It's another night to celebrate, don't you think?" She was pleased at the light, teasing quality of her voice.

He held the wheel easily, negotiating the S curves around the moonlit lake. "I seem to recall losing two shirt studs the last time you decided to celebrate." His voice was husky, amused.

"Did you ever get them back, Alex?"

"Audrey returned them the next day."

He reached for her hand to pull her close. His touch made her skin flame in reaction. She couldn't fall under his spell again. She fought him with the only weapon she had—words. "I'm glad. I wouldn't want you to be—incorrect at your next formal occasion."

He had succeeded in pulling her close. Even in the dark, the tight muscle in his lean cheek that quivered in reaction was noticeable to her, but he didn't loosen his grip on her hand. They rode through the night in angry silence. Then with that cool control she knew well, he said in a moderate tone, "What is wrong, Cathy? Cutting repartee isn't your normal style."

She turned to give him a wide-eyed stare that was totally lost on his stony profile. "Are you that familiar with my 'normal style?' "

A slight smile tugged at his lips. "I thought I was."

Her voice was as cool as a summer breeze. "Perhaps you were mistaken."

Outside his house, Alex stepped on his brakes with extra force. She saw Max's car, a long black limousine parked in the extra space. The driver lounged inside, his head back against the seat.

Alex helped her out of the car with his customary courtesy, but his face was remote as they started down the path.

A breeze from the lake lifted her skirt and sent it drifting across to Alex's trousers where it caught and clung. Hastily, she jerked it away.

His reaction was instantaneous. He whirled to her and gripped her upper arms to stop her forward motion. "I'll ask you once again . . . and I want an answer this time. What in hell is wrong with you?"

"Nothing. What could possibly be wrong? I'm a success—and that's what counts, isn't it?" Her eyes glittered through the night at him.

"At the rate you're going, your 'success' won't last long. You've been in this business long enough to know that temperamental actresses are a dime a dozen. Nobody wants them—especially Max. He runs a mile from any female with an inflated opinion of herself."

"And we mustn't offend Max, must we?" she asked sweetly.

His face darkened ominously. But whatever words he might have said were halted by the opening of the door.

A rotund man in a brown suit stood in the entryway, a glass in his hand. "I thought I heard voices. Come in, come in, Alex," the man invited. "Can I get you a drink?" A gleam of mischief shone in his brown eyes, his shoulders moving as he chuckled at his own joke.

"I'll fix my own, Max," Alex said brusquely. "Cathy?"

"Nothing for me, thank you." She refused to acknowledge the eyebrow he lifted in mocking amusement at her.

"Yes," Max Bernstein said, turning his round head to Alex, as if they had just been talking, "I see what you mean."

"Has Mr. Reardon been saying things about me?" she asked lightly, perching on the stool next to the snack bar.

Max Bernstein studied the amber liquid in his glass. "Having only seen you made up as a young girl, Ms. Taylor, I questioned your—allure as a young woman. Alex informed me you were quite . . . beautiful." Before she could catch her breath, he lowered the glass. "I've already seen what power you have over an audience, Ms. Taylor. I want you for my next play," a smile lifted his lips, "a play that is about as far from Ibsen as you can get."

She braced herself back against the bar and tried to look calm and cool. "What is the story line, Mr. Bernstein?"

"You play a young lawyer—who falls in love with the man she is representing in the trial for the murder of his wife."

"Sounds very—intriguing."

"Most people think so." The sharp eyes played over her. "I wanted an unknown, a fresh face who would be totally believable and tug at the heartstrings of the audience."

"And you think I can do it?"

His eyes lowered slightly. "I'm sure you can—with Alex's direction."

She was riveted with shock. "Alex will be directing?"

"Of course. Well?"

A mixture of excitement and fear clawed at her stomach. "I don't know what to say . . ."

"You don't know what to say?" Max Bernstein echoed in astonishment. "Why, you must say yes, of course!"

A quick look at Alex's impassive face told her nothing. "I'm not sure I'm capable . . ."

"Nonsense. Of course you are." The small eyes in the round head gleamed over her. "My dear young woman, most actresses would give their eye teeth for such an opportunity. I don't understand your reluctance. With Alex as director and me as your producer—you have absolutely nothing to worry about."

Nothing to worry about! There was an understatement. She shook her head, unable to speak.

Bernstein frowned and glanced at Alex. "Haven't you discussed this with her at all?"

"I didn't want her to be prejudiced in advance," was the cool answer. "She has to do what is best for her."

Max Bernstein turned back to Cathy. "Well, now that you know you will be working with Alex, surely your answer is yes, no?"

"Don't badger her, Max." The words were clipped.

"Badger, badger, who's badgering? You told me the girl was

wonderful, I saw for my own eyes the girl is wonderful. But is she willing, that's what I need to know."

She was already confused and Max's words didn't help. She couldn't seem to sort out any thoughts in her head at all. Only one thought surfaced. She was being handed the opportunity of working with Alex—and seeing him—for the next several months.

But being with him—how? As his leading lady lover? To be tossed aside when the play was over? Or suppose Alex grew tired of her and turned his attentions to another woman in the cast? Could she bear to stay on—seeing him every day, knowing he was lying in the arms of another woman?

But there was the matter of her career. This was what she had always dreamed of, a long-term assignment on Broadway. Any other actress would have killed for the chance, as Max had said.

But it was risky, oh dear God, it was risky. Even if the play failed, she would still be working in close proximity to Alex for the next six months.

But she couldn't refuse. She'd been working for a chance like this all her life. Looked at clearly, coolly, logically, there was no choice. She had to take her courage in hand and not think about the consequences. She would have to accept Max's offer—and worry later about how she would deal with her own emotions.

She straightened. "When do I report to wardrobe, Mr. Bernstein?"

His round face broke into a smile. "The fifteenth of September, Ms. Taylor . . ."

"I'll be there."

Max Bernstein lifted his glass. "To our continued association. May it be long and lucrative." He took several noisy swallows and then leaned forward to place his glass on the low table in front of the couch. "Excellent bourbon, Alex, I thank you. Now, I must leave. My driver doesn't like to be kept waiting." When Alex moved forward, he held up his hand. "No, don't bother to see me to the door. I'll see you both in New York on the fifteenth."

He was whistling an off-key tune as he went out and closed the door behind him.

Achingly aware of the intimate quiet in the house, and the trees sighing outside, she slid off the stool. "I suppose I'd better be going . . ."

"Why?" The word was lazy, huskily suggestive.

"Because it's late and I—"

He was beside her, stealing her breath with the look in his eyes. He raised his hand and laid his fingers on the delicate skin at the side of her neck just above the yellow collar. "Are you planning to meet Carson somewhere?"

She stared at him in consternation. "No, why would I do that?"

With only the slightest change of pressure in his fingertips, he drew her closer. "You were kissing him in the parking lot."

"I was wishing him good luck," she said huskily. At the feel of his mouth on her temple, her skin tingled with pleasure.

Her breathy whisper seemed to please him. Some of the tension went out of his body and he pulled her closer—making her level of tension soar. She could feel the smooth material of his jacket and smell the musky male smell of him mingling with his wood-scented cologne. "Wish me good luck, Cathy," he ordered softly.

"You don't need luck," she denied his request in the same soft voice. "You have everything you need—intelligence, fame, talent, courage . . ."

"I don't have an umbrella for a rainy day," he murmured, his words bringing back in a sensual flood the remembrance of that day they had made love. His onslaught on her senses continued as his lips began a slow journey over her cheekbone to the delicate shell of her ear.

"It isn't raining . . ."

His hand wandered to the back of her hips and he pressed her closer. "Then let's do a rain dance." He began to sway, holding her.

They drifted around the floor, her body melting into his. Her hands slid under his jacket and moved upward over the silk of his shirt.

With a sudden piercing clarity, she knew this would be the last time she would be with Alex like this. When they went to New York, he would be immersed in a new show, new people, and a faster, more hectic environment. Their love affair would be over. A sick, almost dizzying pain swept over her, followed by a determination to savor every moment of this evening to its fullest. As she had that night of the dance, she loosened her hand from his and slid it up the smooth material of his lapel to clasp her hands together at his nape. She arched her back to press her hips against him and looked up into his face.

"My rain dance seems to be having the desired effect," he murmured softly in her ear. He grasped her hips to hold them in the intimate position she had initiated.

"It's not raining." Her husky whisper contradicted him.

"I didn't say it was." He laughed softly in her ear. "I said it was having the desired effect." His leg moved sensuously between the chiffon skirt and her thighs as they danced in slow steps around the floor.

"You wouldn't by any chance be trying to seduce me, would you, Mr. Reardon?" she asked sweetly, another arching movement of her body brushing her breasts against his chest.

His low half-growl answered her. "It's a question of who is doing what to whom. You haven't had wine tonight, Cathy. You have no excuse."

But she did have an excuse. The best excuse of all. She loved him.

"I don't need an excuse." She caressed his neck and her light teasing mood vanished. "I need—you."

He stopped dancing and moved away slightly to look at her for such a long moment that she thought he must be going to refuse her. Then his eyes glittered and he pulled her into his arms. "Did it cost you a great deal to say that?"

His mouth was discovering the sensitive cord of her neck. She tilted her head back to give him greater access, her dark hair falling down her back, her skin on fire with the sweetness of his mouth. *Too much,* she thought, *far, far too much,* and her thoughts merged into speech.

He kissed the muttered words away from her lips and his hands went to the back of her dress. He was stilled with reaction. "Good God."

His fingers went over the tiny buttons with their silk loops. "There must be a million of them," he murmured into her neck on a husky breath of laughter.

"It's a designer dress," she murmured.

"It must have been designed by a woman."

She shook her head. "It's a Robert Blake . . ."

He moved away and she made a small sound of distress. He reached for the lamp switch and the next instant the room was plunged into darkness. The moon shone through the trees, casting shadows on the lawn and turning the lake into a gleaming silver surface. He came to her and took her in his arms. His hands went around to her nape and brushed aside her hair.

"Alex—in the dark, it will take forever . . ."

"Your impatience is flattering, my love." He unbuttoned a button and brushed his lips over her temple. Another button came loose and a butterfly kiss teased her cheekbone. With each button, his mouth touched another place on her face. When enough buttons were loosened to slide the dress over her shoulders, he kissed the creamy flesh in a slow, leisurely path to the top of her breasts. The dress fell to the floor. His hands guided the slip straps over her shoulder. "Yes," he said, "only a man would know how enticing a woman's flesh is when it can be seen and not touched."

The slip followed her dress. Her body was kissed and caressed as he removed her lacy underthings.

"Now it's your turn."

She stood in the darkness, her pale body gleaming. Her fingers trembling, she began to unbutton the silk shirt.

When she had undressed him completely, she could only stare at the male beauty that emerged, the strength and virility of him.

"Alex," she whispered softly, "Oh, Alex."

They sank to the rug together and there in the moonlight, he rediscovered the wine-dark sweetness of her mouth, the smooth taut flesh of her breasts, the silken beauty of her thighs. She gloried in his searchings and sought her own pleasure, running her palms over the hair-crisp skin of his chest down to the hard bones of his lean hip.

How bittersweet it was to make love to him again and know that this would be the last time she would lie in his arms! His hands and mouth on her skin raised her to a frenzy of wanting. With her lips and body, she told him of her need. He answered her at last and moved over her to make her his in sweet, total possession.

She lay in the drugged aftermath, not wanting to move. Alex was beside her, a warm hand curved over her hip.

"I'd better go," she murmured.

He lifted his head and buried his mouth in the curve of her neck. "You're not going anywhere—except up to my bed."

"I can't stay—"

"You can, and you will." He rose. "Give me your hand, Cathy."

His lean body was outlined against the light from the windows. He extended his arm to her. In a slow motion dream, she reached for his hand. He pulled her up and into his arms, his naked body against hers wakening her desire to new life. He broke his embrace enough to push her toward the stairs. She walked beside him, unbearably conscious of his hip moving beside hers.

At the top of the stairs, he led her to the bed and pulled back the covers. "Get in."

She lay down on the silken sheet and the bed dipped as he moved in beside her. Gently, he turned her to nestle her against his chest and buried his face in her hair. "Sleep, first, Cathy."

"And then?" she murmured huskily, her back and hips feeling the hard, male imprint of his body.

There was laughter in his voice. "I'll let you think of something."

Just as the sun was coming up, he woke her, and they made love in the early dawn with the smell of the dew on the grass drifting in the windows, and the first song of the birds in her ears. He kissed her to sleep, and when she came awake the second time, the smokey-sweet smell of bacon teased her tastebuds and the light of the sun played over a tousled bed that was empty of Alex.

A trip to the bathroom rewarded her with the gray silk robe. She slipped into it, tied the belt around her waist and went down the stairs.

Alex was in the kitchen, whistling in an expert fashion. He looked up, his eyes caressing. "Good morning."

"Good morning." She stood watching his deft movements as he made toast and poured the orange juice. He looked up from his work. "Sit down. You've timed it perfectly."

The steaming hot coffee had an enticing fragrance. Everything was perfect—too perfect. How many times had he done this before? Was it simply a scene he did over and over? Find a woman, make her a star, make love to her, feed her breakfast? Send her on her way?

He set a plate of eggs and bacon in front of her, his short-sleeved T-shirt exposing the play of muscles in his arms as he moved. He wore a pair of old jeans, laundered to a body-fitting comfort.

"I must say that robe looks far more fetching on you than it does on me." He sat down across from her and smiled.

"Perhaps it depends on your point of view. I rather liked you in it," she said daringly, her eyes moving over him.

He shot her a dark, warning look. "Eat your eggs, Ms. Taylor and don't provoke me—or you'll find yourself back upstairs in that bed in two seconds flat."

The thought of those passionate moments of last night made her wince inwardly. She would never again experience his lovemaking. She fought the tormenting thought with light words. "You could serve me breakfast in bed, then. Perhaps you ought to consider adding that to your repertoire, Alex. Your next leading lady would adore it."

His hand, holding a fork, was stilled. "What exactly do you mean by that?"

She met his eyes with a bravado she didn't feel. "I don't want you to think I've attached any—special importance to the time we've spent together, Alex. I know that when we go to New York—" she stumbled on, the pain acute, "things will be . . . different."

"Will they."

It wasn't a question, it was a cool, flat statement, and she didn't need to look at him to know that his mouth was tight. Was he angry because she had taken the initiative in clearing the air?

"Do I understand you correctly?" he asked softly, a faint tinge of menace in his tone, "You attach no special—significance—to our—time together?"

He sounded hard and angry and she glanced at him in surprise. "Of course I don't," she said clearly. "Why should I? You've made it quite clear that your emotions weren't involved —and I accepted that."

"And you believe I made love to you—as a matter of course? As I do to all the actresses I work with? Because that's the kind of man I am?"

Put that way it sounded all wrong, somehow. "I didn't mean —"

He didn't seem to hear her. "As long as we're examining motives—" his eyes narrowed, "what about yours?"

The food had turned to ashes in her mouth. "Don't attack me because I've spoken the truth, Alex."

"The truth." The two words had a hollow sound. "You wouldn't recognized the truth if it walked up and introduced itself to you." There was an alien bitterness in his voice. Dry-mouthed, she laid down her fork. "I think I'd better go."

His mouth twisted. "Why? You haven't completed the list of

scheduled activities. We were to go for a morning swim . . . and spend the afternoon in bed." His words sliced and wounded.

"I'd like my clothes, Alex."

His face was wooden. "They're on the couch."

In the end, he had to help her with the buttons. He seemed to take an endless amount of time. She tried to ignore the trembling reaction of her body to his hands on her back. When he had finished and she was dressed, she turned to him. "I'll withdraw from Max's play if—"

"You'll do nothing of the kind," he said stonily. "I told you once before our professional lives have nothing to do with our personal ones." His eyes flickered over her mercilessly and the deep lines on the side of his mouth became deeper.

There was a long, endless silence. Then she said, "Goodbye, Alex. I—wish you luck."

She turned away but his voice prevented her from moving. It was hoarse, tortured and totally unlike him. "So you walk out the door—and you're safe."

She faced him. The mental torment in his tone was echoed in his face.

"Safe?" The pound of her heart seemed to be louder than that one word.

He lifted his arm in an eloquent gesture of stage proportions. "Safe, yes. Safe from me."

"I'm not afraid of you." Her eyes locked with his. It was a patent lie. In his denims and T-shirt, his dark chest hairs curling above the round neck, he was more vividly male, more dangerous than ever.

"Yes," he argued softly. "You're afraid because you love me."

"No—" she shook her head, but he took a step closer and she had to fight not to back away.

"Yes," he said again in an even softer, more intent voice. "You love me. You've proven it over and over again. You were afraid to take the part of Hedvig—because you were afraid of failing me."

She gazed at him steadily. "How long have you known that I loved you?"

"Almost as long as I've known I love you." His eyes caught and held hers. "Do you believe me?"

"I want to—but I—"

"Come here," the words were soft, "and I'll prove it."

Joy and happiness exploded in her like a fountain of mist. With it came the knowledge that he was hers to tease, to love, to cherish. She gazed at him, focusing all her attention on appearing serious. "Perhaps . . . if you asked me nicely . . ."

"Come here, woman." He lounged against the couch, waiting.

"I'll meet you halfway." A gleam of mischief escaped her control over her facial expression.

"And not an inch more, I suppose," he murmured.

She shook her head. "Not even a centimeter." She stook a step forward. He made an impatient sound and in two swift steps was in front of her, clasping her in his arms. His voice in her hair was muffled. "My God, Cathy. Do you know what it did to me when I thought you were going to walk out that door?"

By that same magic he always seemed to cast over her, he had turned her and was guiding her up the stairs. "Yes, Alex, I think I know how you felt. Because I felt exactly the same."

"Then why? Why were you going to leave?"

She followed him upward, step by step. "Because I wasn't sure of you—or myself. I wanted you to love me because I'm me, not because I'm an actress. But Alex, if you knew—"

He led her to the bed, pulled the covers back and pushed her down to its silky sheets. He followed her down, his weight an erotic pleasure on her breasts. "And have you more in a state of panic than you were already about your role in the play?" He shook his head. "No. I couldn't take the chance of jeopardizing your career. I knew Max would make it up here eventually. I wanted him to see you as you were. And he did. Max knows a good thing when he sees it," his tongue found her earlobe, "and so do I. I know an exciting, desirable woman when I see one—and—" his hands wandered to her back—and then he groaned.

"My God. Those damned buttons."

She laughed up into his face. He leaned over her, his eyes caressing her. He said, "It doesn't matter. We'll have the rest of our lives to unbutton buttons. Marry me, Cathy."

Her slow smile was like the tip of an iceberg that only showed the edge of her happiness. "Perhaps I will—if you ask me nicely . . ."

He made a soft despairing noise in his throat and lowered his mouth to hers. "I'll have to think of a way . . ."

LOOK FOR NEXT MONTH'S
CANDLELIGHT ECSTASY ROMANCES ®